THE AMISH POTATO FARMER'S WIDOW

EXPECTANT AMISH WIDOWS BOOK 17

SAMANTHA PRICE

AMISH ROMANCE

CHAPTER 1

"I WAS a wandering lost soul until Malachi found me. Through him, I found out what's important in life. I cried out to know the meaning of life one morning, and that very day I met Malachi. It was all meant to be because I hated everything about my life and had nothing to live for. The straw that broke me was when the tire of my car blew out when I was escaping from my abusive ex-boyfriend." She gave a little giggle as she remembered how Malachi had looked, coming along in his buggy, smiling without a care in the world. "Malachi found me crying there by the roadside. I fell in love with him immediately." She stared at the coffin on the other side of her living room. Bishop Luke's wife was one of the few people who hadn't already heard her story that day.

"You'll miss him. Everyone will," Ruth said.

Jeanie nodded. "There is no one like him." Jeanie nibbled on a fingernail and was grateful her mother-in-law was at the door greeting late-comers to the viewing prior to the funeral. Jeanie wasn't herself and now with Malachi gone she never would be. The preparation for the funeral and organizing the food for the meal afterward had kept Jeanie from thinking too much about her loss.

The only thing that mattered was doing what Malachi would've wanted and that was to look after his mother, Magda, and his younger brother, Werner. The four of them had lived together in the old house on the potato farm. They'd all worked hard on that farm for the past years.

When the bishop's wife excused herself and left Jeanie alone, she felt someone standing beside her. She turned to see Amos. "Hello. Have I told you how lost I was when Malachi found me?"

"*Jah,* twice this last week."

"Oh, I'm sorry." She shook her head and looked back at the coffin. It seemed she was in a dream. Ever since she'd been told there'd been an accident she'd felt like she was in a different reality. Nothing seemed real anymore. If it weren't for the other loved ones Malachi had left behind, she'd surely sit in a corner somewhere and do nothing. "I keep thinking I'll wake from this bad dream. I just can't believe he's gone."

"No one can. He's left a big hole in your life — in all our lives."

Jeanie didn't care much about anyone else or what they felt, not today. Her life as it was had ended the day Malachi's buggy had overturned after that collision with the car. The driver of the car had also died and it was determined later he'd been highly intoxicated.

Amos touched her arm lightly. "Today's not the day, but I will talk to you soon about the farm."

Jeanie gulped and stared up at Amos. Was he still going to stick to his agreement about the farm? "We'll continue working as we've always done. The three of us will work harder to make up for Malachi being gone."

His face went stiff, almost like Ruth's face just now when Jeanie realized she'd been talking too much. "We'll speak about it another time."

She turned her shoulders slightly to face him properly. This man held the future of her loved ones in the palm of his hand. "When?"

He blinked his dark eyes. "When you're feeling better."

"I won't recover from how I'm feeling, but I do

have an obligation to others and need to know your thoughts on the farm. Are you still —?"

He pressed his lips together, and said softly, "I'll come see you tomorrow."

"Nee." If the news was bad, she wanted to break it to Werner and Magda herself. It would be easier coming from her. And, there was a better chance of talking him out of bad news if she was by herself. "Can I come to you tomorrow at about ten?"

"Jah. Okay."

That pleased her. Her old *Englisch* life flickered in front of her. Before she met Malachi, nothing had gone right for her. She'd just driven away from a cruel and violent man after having found out he was on the run from the police. She had no family to speak of, and what little she had didn't want her around. What would she do if that pattern of things returned? The worst thing would be if they were all turned out of the house and Amos sold the farm. They had a little savings, but not enough to buy such a farm and he might not be willing to sell it.

"Are you sure you're okay?" he asked.

She'd never be okay again. *"Jah,* I'm all right."

"We'll talk tomorrow." The corners of his lips turned upward.

"Denke, Amos."

Magda came hurrying over as soon as he walked away. "What did he say?"

"We're going to talk about the farm tomorrow. I'm going to his place."

Her green eyes opened wide. Malachi's eyes had been similar to his mother's, only darker. "I'll come too." Magda was the dominating matriarch, but Malachi had still managed to have the rule of the house. Now, Jeanie felt she had to take over that role and lead them. Her first job was to secure their future with what was to be Malachi's.

"*Nee,* Magda. I'll go alone."

She frowned and lines appeared across the bridge of her nose. "Why?"

"I don't want you to be upset if it's bad news."

Magda shook her head. "We were once so close, our family and Amos. Things changed when that woman came into his life."

Jeanie knew she was talking about Zelda. "Everything will be okay. It's got nothing to do with Zelda. I've already told him we'll be able to do all the work. We can employ more helpers than we do now if we can't handle the workload in the busy times."

"*Jah,* but Amos had a special relationship with Malachi and that's why he said he'd make a gift of the farm to him. They were like brothers."

"I'm Malachi's widow and Malachi was

5

supporting all of us. Surely Amos will feel an obligation to look after those Malachi's left behind? The right thing for Amos to do is keep his word to Malachi by transferring the farm to me, to us. It's Werner's legacy too. I'll point that out to him. Anyway, we shouldn't be talking about this right now."

Magda shook her head. "That's the *Englisch* way of thinking, legacies, and such."

"*Nee*. It's the normal way of thinking. Everyone likes money. It makes the world go 'round. Everyone needs it to survive." Just because she wasn't born Amish didn't mean she didn't understand them. She'd made steps to convert not long after she'd met Malachi. The bishop had allowed her to stay with a family until she was sure she could live their ways. After her baptism into the faith, Malachi had proposed to her and she'd accepted without hesitation.

"We shouldn't be worried about all of this today. He should've already told us he'd stick to his word." Magda stared across the living room at Amos who was now talking to Zelda.

Neither Amos nor Malachi had thought about an alternate plan for what would happen in the case of an untimely death. "He just should've given it to Malachi. Why make him jump through hoops like he was a child? He should've known Malachi would make the farm prosper."

"Shh," Magda said. "It was just the way they always were with each other," she whispered.

Jeanie blew out a deep breath. "Okay. You're right. We need to push it from our minds today while we're saying goodbye to Malachi." Jeanie looked over at Zelda. How much influence did Zelda have over Amos? It was odd they hadn't married yet. She had come to this community from one in Ohio just over a year ago and at every meeting since, everyone had expected to hear their marriage announcement. It had never come.

At first, Zelda had stayed with the Harbingers and then she'd rented a small house of her own. Conveniently for her, the house wasn't far from Amos's. Even though Zelda was not someone Jeanie got along with very well, she felt sorry for the woman waiting around for Amos to propose. The rumor was he was the reluctant one in the relation-ship. Zelda looked up at her and Jeanie shifted her gaze elsewhere.

AT THE GRAVESIDE it hit Jeanie hard. He wasn't coming back. Malachi had been her whole world and now she had to find a way of living without him.

That seemed impossible. There was no choice, he was gone and that was that. In despair, she watched the coffin being lowered into the ground. A week ago, he'd left to go into town — a trip she usually made every Tuesday to collect the earnings from their produce at the markets — and that was the last time she'd seen him alive.

When the coffin was at the bottom and the men released the ropes, it was a hard thing to watch.

She felt as though the rug had been pulled from beneath her. Malachi had been her foundation, her rock. Now she was sad, feeling desperately alone, but not broken. The one thing that kept her going was the potato farm. She couldn't even think what they'd do if they didn't have that to work on. It had consumed their lives for years and had been what they'd woken for every day.

Seventeen-year-old Werner touched her arm. He looked just like a younger version of her husband, yet Malachi had been loud and boisterous, whereas Werner was quiet. "You okay?"

"I am." A cold gust of wind swept over her, nearly blowing off her black over-bonnet. She grabbed it and held it in place.

Then she looked up and saw everyone moving away. She stepped closer to the grave and looked down at the coffin in the carefully dug earth. This was one thing out of her control. Death was beyond anyone's control. *I will see you soon, my love,* she said in her head as she stood with Werner.

"Can I just stand here a moment? I know Magda's anxious to get back to the *haus* to help with the food, but I just want a moment."

"Sure. Do you want me to leave?"

"Nee. You can stay by my side."

He smiled and gave her a nod. She looked back at the coffin.

One thing she couldn't understand was how this could fit into God's plan. Why did He take Malachi when he was so healthy and well? He had so much more life to live. It didn't seem fair if life was a lottery, a spin of the dice. "How does *Gott* decide who lives and who dies?" she murmured.

"We don't know. His ways are higher than ours. No one knows the mind of *Gott."*

She hadn't realized she'd spoken her thoughts aloud and was shocked when she heard the booming voice of the bishop behind her. She turned to him. *"Jah,* but … he was so young, so strong. He had so much more living to do. We need him still." Jeanie's stomach ached over the loss.

The bishop shook his head. "I know. I know."

She raised her hand to her mouth and bit into her knuckles to stop herself from screaming. Walking away and leaving Malachi in the ground would be the hardest thing she'd done. "He lies here lifeless. Why? He had everything to live for." She turned, took a step closer to the bishop, and said quietly, "I was the one who was supposed to make that trip into town. He went in my place because I wasn't feeling well. I go there every Tuesday, to the markets to collect our money from the vegetables we grow besides the potatoes. Do you see why this is so awful?" She wasn't sure if she was making sense and felt badly when Werner slowly walked away leaving her alone with the bishop. Was he embarrassed by her emotion?

"He's gone home. He's at peace."

He was at peace here she wanted to scream. "Why didn't *Gott* take me?"

"What made him go instead of you that day?"

"I wasn't feeling that good, that's all, so he said I should rest."

The bishop shook his head. "You don't think *Gott* can take His *kinner* home in a million different ways? He is the Almighty."

She stared into the bishop's light blue eyes. He had a point. "I just feel so wretched. I don't know what to do with myself. I just don't. How am I to go on without him?" She looked into the distance at Magda waiting next to the buggy. Magda had lost a son, but she was taking the loss much better. It was her strong faith, knowing where her son was and knowing it was all in His plan, all according to His will.

"It'll take time," the bishop said.

Jeanie saw Werner had reached the buggy and was now talking with his mother. "This is the second son Magda's lost."

"*Nee,* not lost, Jeanie. The second son to go home before her."

Jeanie blinked back tears. If she thought of her husband as being with *Gott* in heaven surrounded by people he knew, including his older *bruder,* who'd been taken as a child by fever, that eased her pain. She sniffed. "I'm okay now. He's with his *bruder,* isn't he, and with his *vadder?*"

"He is. He's with all those who've gone before. Let *Gott* be your comfort. Turn to Him in times of trouble."

"He's what's kept me going, and being there for Magda and Werner. I know they're devastated. *Denke,* Bishop Luke."

"I'll stop by with Ruth and see you all tomorrow."

"Oh, you aren't coming back to our place now?"

"We are, but we'll also come tomorrow when there aren't so many people around."

"That would be nice."

He nodded and smiled, then walked away. Jeanie looked back at the coffin and out of the corner of her eye, she saw two men with shovels waiting to fill in the grave. "Goodbye, my love. I hope you're happy where you are. I will keep the farm for Werner and your *mudder*. We'll carry on what you started." She sniffed, swallowed hard, and walked up to Magda and Werner just as a beat-up old car slowly moved up the road. It must've been parked behind one of the rows of buggies. It was unusual to see a car near the graveyard shared by the Amish and Mennonites.

Once she reached Magda and noticed her pale face, there was no doubt she'd been putting on a brave front and that's why she'd moved away from the grave. Malachi had been buried between his brother, John, and his father. Who could handle the sight of that without breaking? Magda's cheeks were normally ruddy and full, but today, they were sunken in. She looked so much older than her fifty-nine years. Without Malachi, the three of them in their small family were all a little lost.

CHAPTER 2

WHAT DID Bishop Luke say to you?" Magda asked, from the front seat of the buggy as they headed home.

From the back seat, Jeanie leaned over. "He said he's stopping by with Ruth tomorrow." Jeanie didn't even want to think about tomorrow. It was another day without Malachi and now every day always followed a night alone without him.

"Hmm. I'll have to bake."

"Chocolate cake, please," Werner said.

Magda shook her head. "I was thinking of bread. We haven't baked in days."

Jeanie leaned forward so they could hear her better over the sounds of the horse and buggy. "Well, we do need to keep our strength up. We can't fall apart over this. We need to keep strong hearts, bodies and minds to get us through the next few months."

"I'll go to see Amos with you tomorrow, Jeanie," Werner said.

"I'll go alone."

Magda nodded. *"Jah,* she already told me I couldn't come. She's a bossy one."

"Nee, Jeanie, I'm old enough. Some men my age are married, you know."

"I know you're an adult and everything, but I have my own way of doing things. Besides, you should stay for when the bishop and Ruth visit. It would be dreadful if there was only *Mamm* left at home." Those who'd been at the funeral were heading back to their house for refreshments. Some of the ladies had stayed behind at the house to prepare the food. Things were organized so neither Jeanie nor Magda would have to lift a finger.

All the way home, Werner nagged at Jeanie, giving her one hundred and one reasons why he should go with her to see Amos. So good was he at arguing, Jeanie nearly relented a few times, but kept reminding herself to follow her instincts. Malachi had always told her to follow what felt right in her heart. It felt right to appeal to Amos one on one. Maybe Malachi's widow standing in front of Amos would reinforce the promise he'd made to the man who had been like a brother to him.

When they arrived back at the potato farm, one of their community members was waiting to help them unhitch their buggy, but Werner insisted on doing it alone.

Magda and Jeanie left Werner and walked into the house that was now full of people. Jeanie was pleased so many were there to remember Malachi. Well into the evening, she listened as folks told stories about the jokes and pranks Malachi had played on people when he'd been younger. It had gotten him into dreadful trouble more than once.

That night, the same as every other night since Malachi had died, Jeanie stayed up as late as she could to avoid going to bed alone. It was easier to enter her room when she was exhausted, too worn-out to think.

AFTER JEANIE HAD BREAKFAST the next day, she headed to Amos's place anxious to find out what the future was — not only for the potato farm, but for her family. When Amos's uncle died and left him the run-down farm, Amos had been just about to sell it for next to nothing when Malachi urged him to keep it. Malachi went on to tell him it was a valuable piece of land and if worked on properly, it would once again be profitable.

That was when Amos struck him the deal. He offered Malachi the opportunity to live on the farm for nothing and work it, keep the profits and if certain figures were reached, Malachi could have the farm. Those figures had already been reached and the papers had been drawn up and were waiting at the lawyer's office for signing.

Jeanie had often wondered why Amos couldn't have given Malachi the farm outright if he didn't want to farm it himself, but the two of them were always like that. They were always teasing and testing each other, just as brothers would. Making a success of the farm in a certain time period was Amos's test for Malachi. And he'd passed the test and, with his family's help, he'd exceeded the goals Amos had set.

Amos lived alone in what Jeanie considered a storybook house. It was a two-story white house nestled in fields of varying shades of green. It was surrounded by a high white picket fence to keep in his beloved dog, Jasper. When his home came into view, Jeanie knew she'd be annoyed if Amos delivered her bad news. They'd made a working potato farm from a dust bowl within the space of four years.

If he sold it, then where would they live and what would become of them?

Heading up his driveway, her heart sank when she saw a buggy hitched to a dark brown horse. Zelda was there. All that morning when she'd carefully rehearsed what she'd say to Amos, he'd been alone. The last thing she wanted was to have a heartfelt conversation in front of a woman who sent prickles up her spine. There was no doubt Zelda would continually have her say and give her opinion.

When she got down from the buggy, Amos came to greet her with Jasper by his side. As usual, the tall, white and tan mixed-breed dog bounded toward her. "Hello, Jasper." He stopped in front of her and sat for a pat. Jasper was very well behaved whenever his owner was nearby.

While Amos secured her horse, they talked about the weather, and then they walked into the house. It seemed to Jeanie they were both nervous as they were chattering over nothing. Thankfully, Zelda was nowhere to be seen when they sat on the couch in the living room. Jasper sat on a rug by the fire and then lay down.

Because Amos hadn't mentioned the farm, Jeanie knew she'd have to be first to do so. She cleared her throat, and began, "Amos, I'm here about the potato farm. I'm just wondering if you're going to have those papers redrawn in my name, or our three names." She paused for a breath. "Magda, myself and Werner." When he just stared at her, she knew he had other plans. "Or, even just in Werner's name?"

"I have to make a decision. It won't be an easy one."

CHAPTER 3

J EANIE SWALLOWED HARD. It was as she'd
feared. "To my way of thinking, you made the
promise to Malachi, so —"

"Don't say anything, please, Jeanie. I've given this
a lot of thought over the past days. This is my idea."
He cleared his throat. "I will buy the three of you a
haus to live in and take back the potato farm."

She gulped. "That's very generous about the *haus,*
but what would you do with the farm?" She knew
the potato farm with its acreage was worth more
than just a house, but it wasn't the monetary value
she was concerned with. The promise he'd made to
her husband was what worried her.

"Zelda wants to have her brothers run it. Then
they can move here to this community."

Jeanie couldn't believe what she'd heard. What

19

did the farm have to do with Zelda or her brothers? "What do they know about potatoes?" She knew the answer — a big zero.

"The same as Malachi knew when he started. Look, I know how hard you and everyone else have worked on the farm and that's why I'm willing to buy you a *haus* in exchange. As compensation, if you will. One of your choice."

"As I said, it's very generous and I'm grateful, but is there some way we can work it out so I can buy the farm from you? You were just about to sign it over to Malachi." She tried to keep her tongue in check, but she couldn't help saying, "It really has nothing to do with Zelda's brothers. This is the first I'm hearing about them."

He rubbed his chin. "I'm in a difficult position."

Obviously, Zelda was in the midst of this. "Is that Zelda's buggy outside?"

"*Jah.* She's in the backyard."

"Oh." She nodded, and knew Zelda was waiting until she left so she could celebrate the good news with Amos. Jeanie and her family would be tossed from the farm and Zelda's brothers would be the ones to prosper from her late husband's years of toil and sweat. "It's like this, Amos. In the first two years, we made next to nothing, it's only in the third year we were able to turn a profit once we knew what we were doing. What would've happened if Malachi had lived? He would've had the farm by now."

He rubbed his forehead. "I thought you'd be happy with what I've offered. Don't you see that things won't be as easy at the farm with him gone?"

'Easy?' Things were never 'easy' for us. Is that what he truly thinks? Now, Jeanie was upset and a flush of heat coursed through her body. "I don't mean to be rude, but I know the potato farm is worth a lot more than a *haus.*" She had to fight for the farm for the sake of Werner and Magda. Then she shook her head knowing she sounded like she was a money-grabbing person. "It's not the value or the money. It's what we've all worked for. We all worked so hard and … well … especially Malachi. Nothing about the farm has ever been easy, but it was our life's work. We'll continue to make it successful." She fixed a confident smile on her face.

He stared at her. "Why's it so important to you?"

"It's not just me, it's my family."

"Ah, Werner."

"Jah, Werner. It would've been left to him since Malachi and I have no *kinner.*"

"What would you say if I keep Werner on as manager? He can teach Zelda's brothers how to run the farm. He'll have a wage, of course."

That was another insult to her. It was no solution at all. Amos was smiling as though that would fix everything. "I run the farm now, not Werner. He doesn't know everything like I do."

"What he doesn't know, you could teach him, and it's a way of giving him an income."

He doesn't need an income. Not when he could have the potato farm. Was this man really just going to hand over what should've been theirs to Zelda's brothers? She took a couple of deep slow breaths to help her remain rational. Long ago, before she'd met Malachi, she'd had a problem with anger. Waiting a minute or two before speaking was always wise, she'd learned. "So, are you and Zelda getting married or something to give her such a gift?"

He looked away. "I'm fond of Zelda."

From his reaction, Jeanie wondered if he was ever going to marry Zelda, and if it was to make up for her moving all the way from Ohio that he was handing the farm over to her brothers. Did Zelda know what was going on in Amos's head? On the other hand, he could be about to marry Zelda and she was pressuring him to do that favor for her brothers before she agreed to the nuptials.

Jeanie's gaze was drawn to the intricate carving on the legs of the coffee table. It was unusual for an Amish person to have something that wasn't plain.

Everything else in his house had no decoration at all. "That's a nice table."

"Zelda gave it to me."

She frowned, not liking the table so much anymore. She'd never been comfortable around Zelda and she'd struggled with that in the past. Now the woman was becoming a thorn in her side. "I'll be honest with you, Amos."

His eyebrows rose. "I wouldn't want you to be any other way."

"The thing is, I thought you'd honor your agreement with Malachi by signing the farm to me as his rightful heir. I know the contract was never signed, but it was as good as done. Malachi met your criteria and he put his heart and soul into that farm. We all did." She leaned forward. "If he'd lived, he would've gone to your lawyer's office, signed that contract and the farm would be mine right now. Won't you sign the farm over to me? All it would need is to cross out his first name on the contract and write mine in."

With the worst timing in the world, Zelda walked into the room. "A woman running a farm? Don't be stupid, Jeanie!"

CHAPTER 4

PRICKLES OF ANNOYANCE covered Jeanie's body over Zelda eavesdropping on them. She'd been justified in not liking this woman. What did Amos see in her? *"Nee,* Zelda. Why would you call me stupid? Women run farms and businesses all over the place."

"Not Amish women."

"Jah, I'm talking of Amish women. They don't all stay home baking and cleaning anymore while their husbands toil in the fields. This is a new age. Most of the women in the community work outside of the home. They run roadside stalls and sew quilts for the tourist outlets."

"Well, I don't like it and neither does Amos." She sat next to Amos folding her hands into her lap like a prim and proper lady.

By walking into the room, she'd woken Jasper. He

25

raised his head, looked at Zelda with what Jeanie thought was an unhappy look and then he placed his head back between his paws.

Jeanie let out an exasperated sigh and looked at Amos. "Is it because I'm a woman? If I were Malachi's *bruder* would things be different?"

"If he'd signed the contract when he should've we wouldn't be talking right now, but he didn't. The contract was waiting at my lawyer's office for nearly a week." He showed no emotion, simply spoke the words. "My agreement was with Malachi."

"He's no longer with us." Zelda leaned toward Jeanie, sticking out her pointed chin as she spoke.

In shock, Amos stared at Zelda, for the first time showing his disapproval.

"*Jah,* I did notice that," Jeanie shot back. "I know that for a fact every day when I wake up alone."

"You haven't been Amish long enough to know —"

"Zelda, that's enough," Amos said. Zelda stared at Amos as though she were dreadfully hurt.

"You know nothing about me, Zelda," Jeanie said.

"Well, *excuse* me." Zelda rose to her feet and then walked stiffly out of the room.

The two of them sat in silence until they heard the back door close.

"I'm sorry about that, Jeanie," Amos said.

"Don't be sorry. She's only saying what you're thinking. At least she had courage enough to verbalize it." Jeanie stood up and Amos bounded to his feet.

"I don't agree with her."

"Then give the farm to me." When she saw his unchanged expression, she added, "I can pay you off over time. I've even got a small up-front deposit to make."

He hesitated and then looked away from her.

"Do you want to set higher goals for us to reach? As long as they're realistic, we can reach and even exceed them."

He looked back at her. "It's not that."

"Then what is it?"

He placed his hands on his hips. "Zelda expects certain things."

Frowning at him, she tried to keep her voice steady. "Why does the farm have anything to do with her?"

He shook his head. "I know the two of you have never gotten along."

"I don't really know her."

"She said she made an effort to get to know you."

Jeanie shook her head. "Did she now? I don't remember that." It seemed Zelda had been filling his head with nonsense. Zelda had never said two words to her because she kept to herself and rarely mixed with other women. The only female friend Zelda had in this community was Amos's cousin, Veronica. "I have nothing against her, but I was surprised at her attitude just now."

"She has strong opinions on things, I'll give her that."

Jeanie was annoyed that Amos thought highly of Zelda. He must've seen something in her that no one else did. Her thoughts returned to the issue at hand. "What can I do, or say, that will make you happy to sell the farm to me?"

"I know you don't have money enough to do that, Jeanie."

"I can pay for it over time. I can even see if a bank will give me a loan and you can get your money immediately. They probably will when I show them the figures for what we're earning. I've kept the books myself, and you know I used to be a professional bookkeeper before I joined the community, so the books are in excellent order."

"I didn't know that about you. Anyway, there's no need for all that. Leave things with me and I'll give everything some more thought." He rubbed his chin. "Now I'm in a very difficult position, even more so. I didn't know you'd feel so strongly about keeping the farm without Malachi."

"We all do — Magda, me and Werner." She could see the whole thing upset him. Being in the middle like that couldn't have been easy. "Thanks so much, Amos. I hope I haven't made things awful between you and Zelda."

"*Nee*, not at all." He shook his head.

She didn't think that would be true once Zelda heard he was rethinking his options.

He gave her a small smile. "Give me a few days, maybe a week?"

"Okay." She didn't hold out much hope of him changing his mind. Zelda had the advantage of being close to him and would be talking at him constantly, making sure she got her way.

He walked her to the door guiding her gently with his hand on her elbow. "Until then, just keep doing what you've been doing."

"We will." She stepped out onto the porch, and then turned around. "I should say goodbye to Zelda." When his face froze, she knew that wouldn't be a good idea.

"I'll say goodbye for you."

"Thanks." She walked down the steps and headed to her buggy feeling uneasy. Zelda was ready to pounce on the potato farm as urgently as a cat would jump on a mouse. She'd be back in there by now, and ready to fill Amos's head with all kinds of nonsense.

Jeanie patted her horse's neck and when she had collected the reins, she looked back and saw Amos had already closed the door. *All is not lost,* she thought, as she climbed into the buggy. Clicking her horse forward, she told herself she'd had a good result because she'd been able to delay his decision at least for a few days. The only thing was, they'd be living in limbo, still not knowing what was going to happen. Now she had to tell Magda and Werner that nothing had been sorted.

CHAPTER 5

WHEN JEANIE GOT BACK to the farm, Magda and Werner were both standing outside waiting to hear the news. Jeanie stepped out of her buggy and her face must've said it all.

"What happened?" Werner finally asked when his mother said nothing.

"He hasn't decided, but one thing I know is that it's not looking good." Jeanie had thought she'd be able to appeal to Amos's sense of fairness. She hadn't seen herself coming home having to tell them Amos was undecided. It hadn't helped matters that Zelda had been there.

"Tell us what happened," Magda said.

"I don't know where to start." She gave a sigh. "I need a moment to clear my head."

Magda looped her arm through hers. "Come inside. You need *kaffe*."

"I don't feel like *kaffe*. A cup of hot tea would be better."

Werner took hold of the horse's cheek strap. "I'll take care of the buggy. Don't talk about anything until I get there, okay? I want to hear it too, from the beginning."

"*Denke*, Werner. Sure, we'll wait," Jeanie agreed, and together she and Magda walked to the house. Magda made a pot of coffee and a pot of hot tea, and then they sat waiting until Werner joined them.

Werner walked into the house, took off his hat, placed it on the end of the table and sat with them. Jeanie wished she had better news and hoped they could tell by her demeanor that he wasn't giving the farm to them just yet. Nervously, Jeanie took a sip of tea, feeling them both watching her and waiting for her to begin. She set the cup down on the table and took a deep breath. "At first, he said he wanted Zelda's brothers to take over the farm."

"What?" Magda shrieked.

"*Nee!*" Werner was just as shocked.

"It's true, and to make up for it, he said he'd buy us a *haus*."

"Then you should've taken the *haus*," Werner said.

"Did you say we'd take it?" Magda stared at her, her green eyes nearly bulging from her head.

"*Nee,* Magda, we want the farm. I mean, there isn't a *haus.* He said he'd buy one of our choice and he'd take back the farm."

"Doesn't sound like we're going to get it now." Werner leaned back in his chair clearly disappointed with her negotiations. Magda seemed of the same mind.

"We could possibly get nothing now," Magda added. "A *haus* would've been better than nothing, don't you think?"

"Come on, you two. We don't need handouts from Amos. All I want is what rightfully would've been ours if Malachi had signed that contract."

Magda made tsk tsk sounds. "He was always putting things off. They said the ownership paper was ready to sign. He should've gone in to sign it without delay."

"He didn't know he was going to die," Werner said.

Jeanie slapped a hand on the table to snap those two out of their silliness. "Should've, would've, could've, but he didn't. We've got to look forward not backward. I don't want a *haus.* I want the farm. It should be ours."

Magda blinked rapidly. "If he's happy to give us a *haus* why not take it?"

"We have a deposit for a *haus* if we use the money Malachi and I saved. And, Magda, you must have a little money set aside from the sale of the house you were living in before we all moved here?"

"I do. We could put our money together and —"

Jeanie interrupted her. "It's not about that. Besides, we have this *haus* if we can stay here. The point is, sure, we could get by without this farm, but I want what was rightfully Malachi's. He worked so hard for this. He saw it as not only his future but all our futures."

Magda moved uncomfortably in her chair.

"I should've gone with you." Werner shook his head, slumping further into the chair with his hand over his forehead.

"Nee." Jeanie felt awful that they didn't think she'd done a good enough job. Werner was impressionable and young. The last thing she wanted was to disappoint him. "The result wouldn't have been any different if you'd come, and it might even have been worse."

"Things were never the same since Zelda arrived. She changed him." Now Magda was the one shaking her head.

"Let's get back to work and put everything out of

our minds. That's all we can do. We'll leave everything in *Gott's* hands." Jeanie looked from mother to son trying to cheer them up.

"You know what day it is tomorrow?"

"*Jah*, I know, Werner. It's planting day." It was March seventeen, the day on which they planted the crop. It was hard and almost backbreaking work.

Werner groaned. "Is he trying to get the last of the hard work out of us? Is that what he's doing?"

Jeanie sucked in her lips. "He's not like that. He wouldn't know when we plant."

"*Nee,* he's not bad natured, he's ignorant. Ignorant of what it's taken to get this place on its feet. We can't complain about an honest day's work. We have to keep working as hard as we have and never let up until we have to leave. Now, a good meal and an early night is what we all need." Magda gave a nod of her head.

"I am against planting tomorrow."

"Why?" The two women asked as they looked at Werner.

"I think we should wait to plant. We've had a late cold snap and I don't think we're done with the frosts."

Jeanie had to be the one to make the call. "I say we plant."

35

"Nee, I don't think so. It wouldn't hurt to wait a week or so."

"We plant tomorrow and do what we've always done." She saw by Werner's face he didn't like the idea. "We've already got people coming to help, and, if I'm wrong, I'll take the consequences."

Werner shook his head. "We all will. We'll have to pray for mild weather."

"We'll do what you say Jeanie," Magda said.

"All right." Werner frowned, clearly disapproving.

"Now, I've made Malachi's favorite for dinner."

Jeanie was glad that the planting decision was made and Magda was rallying to a more positive mood and trying to drag her son along with her.

"Chicken and asparagus pie?" Werner asked.

Magda shook her head. *"Nee."*

"I know there wasn't time to cook a roast, and I would've smelled it." Werner sniffed the air.

"Wrong. It's plain old beef and bean casserole."

Jeanie had never known that to be a meal Malachi particularly enjoyed, but he did like plain food, such as sausages and mashed potatoes. That was going to be her next guess. Good thing for them they all liked potatoes. There was never any shortage of those. "Did Bishop Luke and Ruth stop by today?"

"Jah, they've been and gone."

"What happened?" Jeanie asked. "What did they talk about?"

"Nothing much. They were only here about an hour. They asked if we needed help with anything and I said we were fine."

"Good."

Over the evening meal, Jeanie told them the rest of what Amos had said about Zelda's brothers running the place and offering to keep Werner on as manager. Werner said he had no interest in staying on and suggested, if the worst were to happen, they'd start afresh somewhere else. The three of them all agreed that's what they'd do.

CHAPTER 6

THEY HAD extra hands arranged for the next two days to plant all of the fields. During those two days there was no sign of Amos. He hadn't come to see how they were getting along on at their busiest time of year apart from their harvesting days.

Not long after breakfast the day after the planting was completed, Amos came to the house. Werner was in the fields checking on things and Jeanie was heading out to join him when she saw Amos's buggy approaching. "Put the teakettle on, Magda. We have company."

"Who is it?" Magda's head appeared at the kitchen window.

"It's Amos." Jeanie went out and waited for him at one side of their driveway, the side near the hitching post. When he got closer, she searched his face to see if he had good news for them or bad.

He raised his hand in the air. "Hello."

"Hi, Amos. It's good to see you." *If you have good news, that is,* she felt like saying.

He stepped down, secured the buggy and then slowly walked over to her.

"Magda's just put the kettle on. Care for a cup of *kaffe?*"

"Jah, denke."

The only thing she sensed from him was the tension he was covering with too big a smile. She didn't know whether things would go right or wrong. "Magda's in the kitchen. Shall I fetch Werner too?"

"Nee it's not necessary."

There was an awkward silence as they walked. "How's Zelda?"

"I haven't seen her for a few days. She was okay then."

"Oh, good." That meant she hadn't been in his ear continually, trying to sway him one way or another.

They walked into the kitchen and Magda greeted him and pulled out a chair. "Here. Sit in this one."

He chuckled. "Okay. Why this particular one?"

"It's just that from there you can look out the

window and see all our hard work." Magda bent down beside him once he was seated and pointed outside.

"Ah, that's right. You've done the planting."

Jeanie sat next to him. "It's all done."

"Hot tea or *kaffe*, Amos?"

"Just a half a cup of black *kaffe, denke*, Magda."

Magda placed a plate of sliced fruitcake on the table and then proceeded to make the hot drinks.

"Have you decided what you want to do yet — with the farm, I mean?" Jeanie figured the straight-forward approach the best one.

"I'll wait until Magda sits down with us."

"Of course." Jeanie watched Amos as he looked over the fields and hoped he was thinking what a marvellous job they'd done.

When they all had their hot drinks and Magda was seated, he took a slow sip of coffee and then placed the mug back down on the table. It felt like ages before he spoke. Jeanie and Magda looked at one another waiting for him to say something.

"As long as the three of you can manage the farm the way you have been, I am inclined to leave it in your capable hands."

Jeanie sprang to her feet. "Really?" He raised a hand and she slowly sat again, dreading what was to come. She knew there was more.

SAMANTHA PRICE

"I've decided to reassess the situation in six months."

Jeanie slumped down. "What does that mean?"

"I don't want to rush into any decisions. I've got two lots of people in my life who each want me to do different things with this place. I'm torn." The faint lines in his forehead deepened.

"Do what is right," Magda said.

"I don't know, Magda. What is right? The farm is mine, and yes, I pledged it to my friend, but now he's gone. He didn't sign the contract and that might have been for a reason, because it's still mine. Maybe it was meant to happen this way."

"Jah, but from our point of view, if he'd gone in and signed those papers —"

He cut Jeanie off. "He didn't though and now I have … he just didn't."

Magda pushed the plate of cake forward to Amos and he shook his head. *"Nee denke.* I've just eaten."

"What do we do now, then?" Magda asked.

Amos smiled at her. "Just continue doing what you've been doing."

"Continue to work hard despite knowing it could be snatched away from us at any minute?" The words slipped out of Jeanie's mouth, but she no longer cared so much if she sounded rude. It was a lot less than she could've said.

42

His dark eyes gazed upon her. "Let's not forget it's my farm to do with what I want."

"Well you can —"

Suddenly, Magda's hand covered Jeanie's just in time stopping her from losing her temper. She'd been about to say some words that Amos had likely never heard before, and certainly not from the mouth of an Amish woman.

Magda said, "We appreciate the chance to keep this place, Amos, we really do. We've worked so hard on it."

"I know, and that's why I offered to buy you a *haus* should I decide to do something else with this place. I thought it'd compensate you for Malachi breathing life back into this farm."

"We all worked on it, not just Malachi," Magda pointed out. "We're a team, and we all worked well with each other. We'll all work harder to make up for one less team member."

"*Jah.* I'm sure."

Jeanie pressed her lips together, surprised at her mother-in-law talking about teams and members. She'd never heard her talk like that before. Amos did have a point about it being his place, but she couldn't get past the fact that it could've been theirs if Malachi hadn't put off going to the law office.

They engaged in small talk for the next fifteen minutes until Amos drained the last of his coffee.

"Denke for the opportunity, Amos. We are grateful," Jeanie finally said when she thought he was nearly ready to leave.

"I just want to do the right thing by everybody."

Jeanie knew he wanted to do the 'right thing' by Zelda. Had he offered the farm to her brothers, or had it been Zelda who'd asked for them to work there? It was odd if she'd asked such a thing seeing their wedding hadn't even been announced yet.

WHEN AMOS LEFT, Werner came running over to Jeanie as she stood waving goodbye. "What did he say?"

"He said we could stay here a while and then …"

"Then we don't know what," Magda added from behind her.

"Oh." Werner looked as though someone had punched him hard, and Jeanie felt sorry for him.

"Things will work out. Just remember that," Magda said.

Werner exhaled deeply. "I guess so."

Magda continued, "If Malachi was here, he'd say things have always worked out for us and they'll continue to do so."

Werner nodded and then walked away dragging his feet as he went. "I hate to see him like that," Jeanie whispered.

"It's hard for all of us not knowing our future, but especially for a young man just starting out."

CHAPTER 7

THE NEXT MORNING, Jeanie woke to Magda shaking her. She sat bolt upright. "What is it?"

"We've had a frost."

Jeanie ripped off the covers and raced to the window. A frost was the very worst thing that could happen days after planting. For as far as she could see the ground was covered in a sparkling white blanket. *"Ach nee!* Does Werner know?"

"Jah, he's the one who told me."

Jeanie felt so bad. "I should've listened to him." She spun around and looked at Magda. "Malachi wouldn't have made this mistake. This is awful." They'd never had a frost after planting; it was a major disaster. They could lose the majority of their crop if not all, especially if it rained as well.

"Why would *Gott* punish us like this?" Magda sobbed and Jeanie quickly put her arms around her.

Magda and Werner had trusted in her decision and she'd let them all down. There was no worse feeling. When Jeanie saw how bad her mother-in-law felt, she searched her mind for what Malachi would've said to cheer her mood. "It'll all work out for the good. Just you wait and see." It was hard saying those things when she didn't believe them.

Magda stared at her. "It's a frost, Jeanie."

"I know. We're not the only potato farm that's had a frost, and we won't be the last. We've had two good years, we can cope with less profits this year."

"It'll look bad to Amos."

"He can't blame us for a frost." He could blame them for not being more aware of the weather conditions. In her haste to keep things rolling she'd acted impulsively.

"He won't look at that. He'll just look at the amount on the ledger."

Jeanie didn't think anything like that would matter, not really. They probably wouldn't even be there when harvest time came. "All we can do is what we can do. Don't be sad."

Magda wiped her eyes and then nodded. "It's just hard, all these bad things have happened. I've been trying to keep myself from falling apart and now the frost has happened I don't have any more left in me to guard my heart against this sorrow."

"I'll get ready and come downstairs."

Tears fell down Magda's face and she collapsed onto Jeanie's bed. "He'll never be back. When will I see him again? I don't want to die soon, but I want to see him again. I can't cope with the ache in my heart for a moment longer." Magda reached out for Jeanie's hand. "What if something happens to you or Werner? I wouldn't be able to go on."

Jeanie patted Magda's hand.

"Calm down. Nothing's going to happen. You can't be so fearful. Trust in God."

Magda nodded. "We used to teach you about God, and now you're teaching us."

Jeanie had to smile as she sat on the bed with Magda. "I'm only telling you what you told me. It's what you know in your heart." Jeanie leaned forward and wiped the tears from Magda's face. "You've been putting on a brave front for us all, haven't you?"

"I tried … I tried to carry on and be strong. It is a comfort to know he's gone home and is with his *bruder,* but I'll miss him so much." Tears poured out of Magda's eyes as she sobbed uncontrollably. Jeanie leaned forward and enclosed her mother-in-law in her arms, remembering Magda hadn't broken down on the day of the funeral or even shed a tear. She'd kept it all bottled in. There was nothing she could say to make her feel better, so she continued to hold her as she sobbed. "I'm sorry. I should be the one comforting you," Magda finally said.

"Nee, nee. He was your son."

"Now I've lost him and we might lose this place."

Jeanie sat straight. "Things will work out. What's the worst that can happen? We lose the farm and then, so what? We'll start again on our own somewhere and make a success out of whatever we do. That's what *Gott's* plan might be. We don't have to hang on to the farm as though this is all we can ever have."

Magda sniffed. "You don't think so?"

In her heart, she desperately wanted to keep the farm. She smoothed some loose strands of hair away from Magda's face. "That's right, so don't you worry about a thing."

"Denke, you've made me feel better."

"That's good. Now how about I make you some breakfast?"

"A cup of hot tea is what I need first."

"I'll bring it up." Jeanie changed into her day clothes, pushed her hair into a *kapp,* and headed downstairs. Werner was nowhere to be seen and at this moment she couldn't have faced him. He had been right about waiting a few days before planting, and she'd been so wrong.

When she placed the kettle on the stovetop, she closed her eyes and asked for extra strength for whatever would come her way.

When she took the tea up to her room, Magda was no longer there, so she peeped into Magda's room. She had fallen asleep on top of her carefully made bed. Jeanie placed the tea quietly on the nightstand and just as she was walking out of the room, a low rumbling sound met her ears. Magda was snoring. Jeanie stifled a giggle as she softly closed the door.

CHAPTER 8

FOR THE NEXT TWO WEEKS, they did what they could to repair the havoc the frost had caused to the newly planted potato crop. Even though they'd never had a disaster so big, every potato farmer had to be prepared for such events. The frost along with Malachi's absence and Amos's indecision, was taking a toll on the three of them.

"Wake up, Jeanie. You're not sick, are you?"

She opened her eyes to see Magda. Then she saw the morning light streaming into the room. *"Nee.* I'm okay. I'm just really tired."

Magda sat on the side of her bed. "I've had the best idea ever. It came to me last night when I couldn't sleep. I was tossing and turning all night because I knew I was missing something."

Jeanie rubbed her eyes. "Missing something? Did

you forget to brush your hair or clean your teeth last night or something?"

"It's no time for jokes. Sit up and listen to me. This is serious."

Jeanie inhaled deeply and then pushed herself up onto her elbows while Magda leaned forward and fluffed up some pillows to tuck behind her. "What are you missing, Magda?"

"I've had the most brilliant idea. You want to keep the farm for us all, *jah?*"

"You know I do."

"The answer is simple. Marry Amos."

Jeanie's mouth fell open and she leaned back into the soft pillows. "Magda, *nee*. Now you're the one with the jokes, but it's too early in the morning to laugh." Jeanie rubbed her eyes wishing she could just have a few moments more in her warm bed.

Magda's face sparkled with enthusiasm. "It's not a joke."

Jeanie shook her head wondering what had come over her mother-in-law. "That's the worst, most ridiculous idea you've ever had, if you're completely serious. I'd rather lose the farm, than marry for anything other than love."

"Ah, but you've had love, haven't you? You'll never find that again. Look at you, you're young, you've got plenty of years to find another man, but he won't be like my Malachi. There are plenty of reasons to marry other than love. Some marry for security. Why not benefit us all and keep Malachi's legacy, as you keep calling it? All you have to do is marry Amos, and he's not even that bad. In fact, he's quite handsome."

Jeanie stared at her and then covered her face with her hands. "Ah, Magda." It was such a dreadful idea and she didn't even know how to begin telling her mother-in-law so.

Magda grabbed both of Jeanie's hands and looked into her eyes. "He was fond of you before you married Malachi, and that spark of interest can be rekindled."

Jeanie cast her mind back. Amos and Malachi were always best of friends, but she'd never noticed Amos was interested in her. "Was he?"

"Jah."

"How do you know?"

"I watch and observe people. Besides that …" she giggled before going on, "Malachi told me that they both liked you. Neither of them did anything about it for some time because they were friends."

"Oh. I thought Malachi stayed away from me when I first came to the community because the bishop told him to."

"That might have been part of it. The bishop

doesn't like sudden relationships when people join us, but it was more than that. When the waiting period had passed, they drew lots on who would approach you first and Malachi won." She let go of Jeanie's hands. "You could very well have married Amos."

She couldn't imagine they would've drawn lots over her. Malachi was known for teasing. He would've told his mother that in jest and she'd taken it seriously. "*Nee.* I'm sorry to disappoint you because that's not how it happened. Malachi found me on the road. I was in love with him from that moment forward. There was never anyone else. So, there was no drawing lots on who would approach me because Malachi and I were always meant for each other from day one. End of story, wrapped up neatly with a pink bow."

"I'm just saying what Malachi told me."

Jeanie rubbed her forehead. "It did take Malachi a while to be romantic with me, and he was always with Amos. They were so close back then."

"You see?"

"I would never have married Amos."

"Maybe not, but …"

"Magda, are you making all this up just to have me throw myself at Amos? What, for the sake of the farm? It's not a life or death thing. We can start over."

"Nee." Magda ripped off Jeanie's bed covers and Jeanie made a lunge forward and pulled them back over her. "Get out of bed now and go see him. This is our last chance to keep the farm."

"What about our talk the other night?"

"I always see things clearer by day," Magda said.

"You're selling me to buy the farm? That's what it sounds like to me."

"You're a beautiful young woman, you'll marry again and he's the best man in the entire region. Don't you think he's handsome?"

"That's not got anything to do with it."

"Is he handsome or not? What do you think?" Magda leaned back and crossed her arms over her chest. "Just answer the question."

Jeanie groaned and then pictured Amos with his chocolatey dark eyes and his glossy dark hair. He certainly was a handsome man. *"Jah,* but Malachi's just gone. It's a little too —"

"Fiddlesticks. I didn't say marry him tomorrow. Get into his heart to start with." Magda pulled the covers off once more and Jeanie pulled her nightgown down over her legs and hugged her knees to her chest.

"I'm cold."

"I'll make you breakfast. Now, get up! Have a shower and freshen yourself up. Put on your best dress and dab some lavender oil behind your ears."

She frowned at Magda. "What about Zelda? Where does she sit with your grand plans? Or did you forget she and Amos might be only days away from announcing their engagement?"

Magda smiled. "I wouldn't be concerned. Zelda can go back home and look after those brothers of hers if she's so worried about them."

"I don't know."

"Just do it. You'll be sorry if you don't. You know the crops aren't going to be good this time around. We aren't going to meet our targets, especially if we have another frost tonight and we very well could."

Jeanie grimaced. "Don't even say it. Okay, I'm getting up."

"*Gut.* I'll see you in the kitchen."

As soon as Magda was out of the room, Jeanie grabbed a towel and headed to the bathroom. While the jets of hot water streamed over her body, she thought more about Magda's plan. Had she really agreed to the madness? What was important right now was for Werner to have a future. The potato farm would've been ideal for him to take over and he seemed in tune with the weather and the earth. More so than even Malachi had been. Werner seemed a born farmer and she shouldn't have told Amos she knew more about the farm than he. Sadly, she'd shown she wasn't as good on the farm as Werner.

Jeanie finished her shower in double-quick time, dressed and fixed her hair, and then headed downstairs.

When she walked into the kitchen, she saw a mug of black coffee, scrambled eggs, sausages and bacon waiting for her. "I can't eat all of that. I'm feeling a bit off. Could you just put a slice of toast on for me?"

"*Nee.* Just eat what you can."

Jeanie slumped into the chair, hating to waste all the food. Magda hadn't offered to eat it, and Werner was always out in the fields early, so she'd have to eat her way through it. "I'll try to eat it all. Now, about this silly plan. You were joking, right?"

"*Nee.* It's the perfect solution."

"Think of it from Amos's point of view. It doesn't matter to me because I've already had love in my life. But, what about Amos? Doesn't he deserve to marry someone who loves him?"

"You'll make him a *gut fraa.*"

"But, love? Doesn't he deserve it? I'm sure Zelda loves him."

"Zelda is seizing an opportunity because he's a wealthy man."

Jeanie looked down at her breakfast and made a start, pushing some egg onto her fork. "You don't think she loves him?"

"I don't know. Probably not."

"How can you say that?" Jeanie popped the egg into her mouth, hoping Magda would see that her idea was a bad one.

"Why has Zelda come here?" Magda asked as she washed some dishes.

"For love?"

"For a better future for her and her siblings, that's why."

Jeanie kept eating while Magda talked. After a while, she saw there was no use objecting. Magda had her mind made up.

"Besides," Magda said, "if you don't think it's honorable to marry him just for the farm and for your future security, don't worry because Amos himself is not being honorable."

"How so?"

"By not signing the farm over to you. It's rightfully yours."

"Hmm. That seems to depend what point of view you have. Anyway, he said that he's giving us six more months. In his mind, he's leaning toward us and not Zelda's brothers."

Magda sat down beside her and stared into her face. "The only problem with your line of thinking is that, with the frost, time is now working against us."

Jeanie looked down at her food. "You want some of this?"

"Jeanie, eat it. Food is the last of our problems."

"I'm just not hungry."

"Forget the food. What do you say about what I just said?"

Screwing up her face, she looked at her mother-in-law. "You're serious?"

"*Jah*. This is the answer. I prayed for the answer and as I was falling to sleep it hit me. I wanted to run into your room and tell you, but I thought you'd be asleep. I waited until morning. Can't you see this will fix everything?"

"So, Zelda can forget Amos and Amos can live a married life without love?"

"*Jah*. Zelda will find someone else and Amos already likes you. I told you that already."

"I can't do it. Just like I can't eat all this." She poked at the food with her fork.

Magda pushed Jeanie's plate aside. "If you think about this with a clear head, you'll see I'm right.

Trust me on this. You're not thinking straight because you're grieving the loss of Malachi."

"And I always will."

"Exactly, so what does it matter who you marry now? Amos is a good man."

"I'm trying to tell you, I'm not thinking of myself. I'm thinking of the two lives that might be ruined if this plan of yours works. It will benefit us but it won't be good for Amos or Zelda. What if they're meant to be together?"

"They aren't. We'll be saving him from that woman, and she'll find someone more suited. Listen to me, Jeanie, if he was in love with that woman, really in love, he would've married her by now."

Jeanie could see Magda had a point. The Amish never had long courtships. It was also quite clear to Jeanie they'd lost their fight to keep the farm because of the damaging frost.

"All right. I'll go see him and then take things from there." She'd humor Magda and go to see Amos.

"Good." Magda got up and took hold of Jeanie's plate. "Take the leftovers to his dog."

"Okay."

"I'll package them for you."

CHAPTER 9

AT MID-MORNING, when Jeanie was heading out the door, she turned to Magda. "Is Werner in on your scheme too?"

"It's not a scheme."

"Whatever it is, does he know?"

"The fewer people who know about this, the better. He left this morning and hasn't been back."

Jeanie knew Werner liked to be out in the fields early, even before the sunrise most times. "Okay. What am I supposed to say when I get there? Aren't I supposed to bring him cake or a pie? Isn't that what older Amish ladies do when they like a man?"

"Hmm. I've been too busy to bake, but you're the one who should've done it by rights if you're trying to impress him."

"I'm not, though." She shrugged. "It'll be odd if I

just show up for no reason, just with a few scraps for his dog." Jeanie wondered if she should go at all. It crossed her mind to only tell Magda she'd gone, but she couldn't deceive her.

"I don't know. You'll think of something on the way. *Gott* will give you words to say if He chooses to bless us in this. If *Gott* is for you, no one can be against you."

"Okay. I hope He gives me words because I have none." She sighed.

"Listen, Jeanie, don't have your face looking so glum when you see him."

"This is the only face I have right now."

"Well, put a smile on it. I'm not sending you to do the worst thing in the world. Women have made plans like this for years. Centuries, even. It's not deceptive."

"I think it is."

Magda's face tilted upward. "There were many cases in the bible of women doing things like this."

"Like?" Jeanie doubted anyone could win through deception.

"Well, there was …"

"Jezebel? She lied and then was eaten by dogs, wasn't she?"

"I wasn't thinking of her."

"Eve? Is that what you're going to tell me?"

"*Nee*. Wait." Magda lifted her hand into the air. "There was Rebecca who got her son Jacob to fool his father into giving him the blessing that belonged to his older brother. His mother had him put animal skin over his arms so his father with his failing eyesight would think he was blessing Jacob's older brother. That turned out well."

"Not for the older brother it didn't, and I recall Jacob didn't have an easy time of things either after that."

"It's the principle of the thing."

"Hmm." Jeanie shook her head. "There seems to be no principle about it."

"Believe in what I say, Jeanie. I had Werner hitch the buggy for you before he left. It's waiting out back."

Jeanie felt she had no choice, and at least she was doing something rather than sitting around moaning about the frost. Now, it was raining, further ruining the crop, and while it was raining, there was nothing they could do. "I'm going." She grabbed her coat and her black over-bonnet. Magda helped her into the coat and then Jeanie pulled the black bonnet over her white *kapp*. She gave Magda a quick kiss goodbye, and headed out the door.

"Wait, Jeanie."

Jeanie stopped in her tracks hoping Magda had

finally come to her senses. "You forgot the dog's food." Magda ran toward her holding up the package containing her leftover breakfast.

"*Denke.*" Jeanie took it from her and continued on toward the buggy.

As her horse pulled the buggy along the quiet road, she wondered what Malachi would think of what she was doing just to keep the farm. He'd only been gone a couple of weeks, and another marriage was the furthest thing from her mind. One thing she knew was there was no one like Malachi. There was a gaping hole in her life and another man wouldn't be able to fill his place. Amos wouldn't see her as a possible wife anyway, she was certain of that. And, if he did, he wouldn't make it known so soon after his good friend's death.

WHEN SHE SECURED her horse outside Amos's home, she ran through a heavier downpour of rain.

Amos flung the door open as soon as she knocked on it. "Oh, it's you." He seemed shocked and there was a certain amount of urgency in his voice.

"Who were you expecting?"

He held his head. "It's raining. Did you get wet?"

She looked down at her dress. It was her best dress, as ordered by Magda. "Not much."

"I'm sorry to sound a little odd. Zelda has just left and gone back to Ohio. I thought she'd changed her mind when I heard that knock on the door."

She reached out her hand and touched his arm. "I'm so sorry, Amos." She'd feel awful if they'd argued over Zelda's brothers not working the farm.

He shrugged his shoulders. "It wasn't meant to be. Are you here to discuss the farm?"

She said the first thing that came into her head. "I heard a rumor she was leaving, so I came to see how you are."

"Nothing stays quiet for long around here." He breathed out heavily.

"You've got that right."

He stepped back. "Come in. Can I offer you tea, *kaffe,* or anything?"

"Just a glass of water please." She heard his dog bark and remembered the food she'd left in the buggy. "I brought some leftovers for Jasper, but I left them in the buggy."

"Denke. We can get them later when it stops raining. Now, your water." He sat her down in the living room and then returned with a glass of water, placing it on the coffee table in front of her.

"It's not over the farm, is it? Is that why she

left?" Jeanie asked. If that was so, then he'd probably leave them with the farm and she wouldn't have to marry him.

"There were other issues."

"Oh, I'm sorry." Nervously, she leaned over and picked up her glass, took a sip of water and then leaned forward again to place it back on the carved wooden coffee table. "I guess you know we've had a bad frost?"

"Nothing that can't be fixed though, right?"

She nodded. "We've done what we can. It's not going to be good. Not as good as last year. There's not much we can do about it while it's raining."

"Why don't we wait and see?"

She smiled at him and because she wanted to keep Magda happy, she tried to remember how to flirt. But, she reminded herself, she might not need to.

"What are you thinking about?" he asked, smiling and appearing more relaxed.

She'd spent enough time in pubs and clubs in her misspent youth to sense he was attracted to her. That was something she'd never noticed before. "I'm thinking about what a good man Zelda has missed out on."

His eyebrows shot up. "I'm hoping she'll return."

"She'd be crazy if she didn't."

His slight smile increased.

"You'd have to be the most eligible bachelor in this whole region. If I weren't in mourning for my dear husband, I might ..." She giggled and realized she was turning back into the old Jeanie of years ago, but he didn't seem to mind. Flirting came natural once she got into the flow. "I should keep quiet."

"It is hard to find someone, a marriage partner, in the community once you're past a certain age."

She nodded. "That's true."

"I'll keep what you said in mind."

It had worked. All she'd had to do was flutter her eyes a little. Surely there was no harm in that?

He swallowed hard. "I hope all this fuss over the farm hasn't caused you too much stress."

"I'd like to say it hasn't, but it has. It's been awful. Especially coming right after Malachi died. I can't be alone." She shook her head as she said the words knowing Magda would've been pleased. "I'm not that kind of a woman."

"I've always seen you as strong. That's one of the things I admire about you."

She nodded. "In some ways, I am, but I believe no man or woman should ever be alone. Wouldn't you agree?"

He settled back further into his chair. "You'll have no trouble marrying again. You have no *kinner*, nothing to remind a second husband of the first marriage you had. Even though he was my best friend, I have to say that a widow free of *kinner* is more appealing to a man and that might be the same for other single men my age."

"We were never blessed with any and I regret that we weren't. I wouldn't say it's a good thing."

"Nee, I didn't mean that. I meant if you were looking for a second husband, a woman just like you would be appealing." It meant the same thing; he'd just reworded it slightly. He licked his lips. "Would it be too soon if you and I spent some time together? Simply for companionship?"

This was moving too fast and she regretted going along with Magda's silliness. She had to get away and come up with a new strategy that didn't involve deceit. "What about Zelda?"

"She chose to leave because she didn't get what she wanted when she wanted it. She was a spoilt child. We've both had recent losses, you and me. We can console each other."

Anger welled within her. Malachi's death couldn't be compared to Zelda walking out on him. "Okay." She fixed a smile on her face and rose to her feet. "I should get back to the farm, so I can work as soon as the rain stops."

He stood. "Before you leave …"

She turned around to face him. *"Jah."*

"You look lovely today."

A girlish giggle escaped her lips. It was a quite an unexpected thing to hear. *"Denke."*

"Do you have some free time on Saturday? There's a piece of land I'm considering buying and I never like going on long car journeys alone."

"You're going by car?"

"Jah, it's forty miles from here, so I've had to hire a car and driver."

Getting out of the area sounded good.

"Come with me. We could have lunch after we see the land."

She had no idea why he was looking at land, and more so, land so far away. "That sounds lovely. What time will you collect me?"

"A little after nine."

She gave him a big smile as she walked out the door. "I'll be waiting."

CHAPTER 10

BACK AT THE POTATO FARM, Jeanie found her mother-in-law in the wet fields. Once she saw Werner was even further in the distance, she stomped over to her mother-in-law. "I can't believe you're making me … sell myself like this."

Magda stood, wiped her brow and then a look of delight covered her face. "It worked?"

"*Jah,* we have a date on Saturday. Can you believe it? A date when I've only just buried my husband." Jeanie shook her head. "He's turning in his grave right now."

"He's not in his grave. He's by Jesus's side looking down on us."

"It's just an expression, Magda, meaning he'd heartily disapprove and I'd rather him not have been looking down on me this last hour. He'd be trying to

73

figure out who this person is that I've become. The worst thing is it might not have been necessary."

"Why?"

"Zelda left him. She's gone."

Magda's mouth dropped open.

"It's true. She left him and she's gone back to Ohio."

Magda's face lit up. "Keep doing what you're doing. She'll be back, and she'll be more forceful than ever if she knows you like him."

"You can't know that."

Nodding, Magda said, "I do. Going away was a ploy. She's pulling on his heartstrings, trying to have him miss her. It was the wrong move for her to make. She should've stayed and put pressure on him."

"Aren't I doing the same thing, putting on pressure?"

"Jah."

Jeanie sighed. "I'll get changed and come back and help you." Exhausted, she fell into the armchair as soon as she entered the house. She'd lost her way and Magda wasn't helping. The fact that she enjoyed Amos's company bothered her and so too did the compliment he'd given her. It was because of those things she felt guilty. It was all wrong.

74

Magda walked into the room and sat down beside her. "The crops aren't as bad as we thought."

"I don't know how that could be true."

"It is, though. Even though Zelda's gone we can't leave things to chance. If you marry him, we'll have what Malachi wanted us to have — a secure future."

"*Gott* is our security. With Him as the center of our lives whatever we do will prosper. We don't need the farm."

"Don't you see that it's *Gott* who's giving us the chance to hold onto it? He rewards those who work for things and those who are diligent." Magda's green eyes widened with intensity.

"Does he reward people for fooling others?"

"Who are you fooling?"

"Amos, of course."

"*Nee,* you'll marry him if he asks."

Jeanie laughed. "I won't. I won't marry anyone else."

"You will. You'll get lonely. That's why I married Werner's *vadder.* It wasn't for love."

She recalled that Werner and Malachi didn't have the same father, but Malachi had grown up with Peter as the only father he'd ever known. "How old was Malachi when his *vadder* died?" She knew he'd been very young.

"Only one."

"That's sad."

"It was, but like everything in life, time eases memories and softens wounds."

"I hope so. I don't want to feel like this forever. I can't imagine things will ever be different. I hope the pain in my heart lessens."

"Trust me, it will. I married a second time to give Malachi a *vadder*. I never regretted that decision and I grew to love him in a different kind of way."

Jeanie shook her head. "I didn't know."

"I never told anyone I didn't love him as much as I did my first husband. It made my life easier too. It was nice for me to have a man to look after." Magda shook her head. "Look at me now. Working hard in the fields."

"You don't need to work hard. We can employ someone else. We have the money to do that."

Magda smiled a little impishly. "I know. I like to do it. It just sounded good."

"Jah, and these days women look after themselves."

"You've still got your *Englisch* mind in there. I said it was nice for me to have a man to look after. I didn't say to be looked after."

"Ach." Jeanie pouted. "I don't think that way …"

"You do. Everyone needs someone and that's all in *Gott's* plan. Every man needs his *help meet.*"

"That may be so. Who knows?"

Magda shook her head at her. "Now, I thought you were coming out to help? We can't let Werner do it all on his own."

"I'm coming. I've been so tired lately. I just need a little rest."

Magda leaned over and kissed her on her cheek. "Don't look so stressed. Everything will work out."

Jeanie nodded. The pair of them were a good team. When one was down, the other managed to pull her up.

CHAPTER 11

"WHY ARE you looking at this land?" It was Saturday and Jeanie stood next to Amos as he looked over the barren landscape.

"Land's getting scarce and this land is inexpensive. They're not making more land you know." He chuckled.

"I guess they're not. Unless we can all move to Mars, or something. This might be cheap because it's in the middle of nowhere and no one wants it. There are no stores, nothing."

He laughed. "All the towns are expanding because of the population growth. And there are jobs in the area."

She curled her lip as he looked away from her. She hadn't seen much expansion going on. Maybe in a hundred years or so, things would expand, but they'd all be dead and gone by then. *"Jah,* but there's nothing around here right now."

"I'll just buy it and hang onto it."

It seemed like a dreadful waste to her unless he was getting it for next to nothing, but it was his money to do with what he wanted. With her hands on her hips, she looked around them once more. "You know something? It reminds me of a potato farm I saw once."

He laughed again. "Your potato farm?"

"Jah, before we made a success out of it."

"Except this piece of land doesn't come with a *haus,"* he pointed out.

"Only because no one wants to live out here."

He chuckled. "With you around, I could save a wagon full of money."

"I guess I'm conservative when it comes to parting with dollars and I don't like waste. I guess that's because of my bookkeeping training with every dollar having to be accounted for."

"I should get you to do some work for me."

She shook her head. "I'm sure you've already got a lot of people much better trained than me looking after your finances."

He smiled and looked around at the land. "There's the southern boundary. That clump of trees by the river. Someday that could be a nice spot for a *haus,* don't you think?"

He liked what he saw. That was obvious by the look on his face. "I don't know without going over there. It seems you already have your heart set on it and you would know more about these things than I do. Don't let me stop you from buying it. You'll blame me if it becomes valuable in a few years. Maybe they'll find oil or gold." She giggled about the wasteland ever becoming valuable.

"We'll see. I'll only buy it if I get it for the right money and with my terms."

The wicked side of her raised its head and she nearly suggested putting Zelda and her brothers out here, but hopefully, that problem no longer existed.

"We should have lunch. Are you hungry?"

"Starving." She had barely touched breakfast but now that empty stomach was gnawing away at her.

The land was so far from where they lived, too far for any horse to get them there. It seemed an expensive day out to hire that big car and the driver, but Amos hadn't flinched about the money.

As they sat in the backseat of the car, Jeanie compared how peaceful it was in a buggy listening to the horse's hooves in comparison to the constant mechanical hum and the speed of the car. She'd forgotten how much she used to dislike riding in a car. The buggy quieted her mind the same way as when she said a prayer. She certainly felt much closer to God in a horse and buggy than she did whizzing about in a car.

"It's nice to get away from the farm and everything." She wanted to say from all the worries and the pressures, until she remembered Amos had caused most of them. Maybe all of them, except for the frosts.

"What would you have been doing on the farm today?"

She'd be at the farm helping Werner do damage control, but she didn't want to focus on that. "Just what I usually do. Working in the fields and then doing bookwork at night. That's what my day usually looks like. Magda helps out with everything and she's the main person who does the cooking and looks after us all."

"It must be hard without —"

"It is hard without him. It is."

"I wasn't going to say, 'Without Malachi.' I'm sorry." He looked down.

"Oh, *nee,* I'm the one who's sorry." Malachi was always on her mind.

"I was thinking you might often consider how much easier things would be with technology if you'd be allowed to use any. With you being raised outside the community."

"Oh." She nodded. "You know, I have never given it much thought. It's been years since I joined the Amish and my old life is so far behind me that I barely remember it." The car pulled up in front of a restaurant. "Is this where we're having lunch?"

"*Jah,* I've been here before. You'll like it."

It looked a little too grand and she knew she'd feel uncomfortable. People would look at them in their Amish clothes and she never liked being stared at. "You've been here before?"

"*Jah.*"

She wondered if he'd been there with Zelda.

IN HER HEART, she felt like she was betraying Malachi, but then she remembered for whom she was doing it. It was for Malachi and his family. She pushed everything out of her mind and focused on Amos. The waitress showed them to a table by the window and Amos stepped forward and pulled out Jeanie's chair.

"*Denke,*" she said, as she sat. He took a seat opposite and then they were handed menus. When the waitress left Jeanie leaned forward. "I feel out of place here."

"Don't worry about it. I felt like that too the first time I came here. Just relax and enjoy the food."

She chose the plainest thing on the menu because she now felt a little wave of queasiness. Or might she just be hungry?

They discussed the food as they looked at the menu, while Jeanie wanted to talk about anything but food. When they'd given their order, he sat and stared at her.

She giggled a little. "What?"

"It's nice to be here with you like this."

"It is good to have a day away from the farm."

He rearranged the items on the table. "Is farm life too stressful for you?"

"*Nee,* I enjoy it. I enjoy watching the crops grow and seeing all our hard work pay off."

"*Jah,* I imagine it would be rewarding."

When their meals came, Jeanie suddenly didn't feel hungry. She thought she'd ordered something quite different. The chicken and mushroom meal was covered in a gravy-like sauce. It turned her stomach. Knowing it cost a lot of money, she knew she'd have to eat it.

"This looks good," Jeanie said, as she picked up a fork.

"Everything I've tried here is good."

They sat, ate and talked for an hour and a half. It

was effortless talking with him except when they were speaking of the farm. It seemed they were of the same opinion about every subject that was mentioned.

WHEN HE BROUGHT HER HOME, she opened the car door. "Are you really going to buy that land?"

"Do you think I should?"

She shook her head. *"Nee."*

"I'll give it some thought. You have turned me off it a little."

Jeanie giggled. "Buy it then or you'll blame me if they strike oil."

He shook his head and grinned. "What would I do with all that money?"

"I don't know."

"I'm happy with my life the way it is. I had a good day with you today, Jeanie. You're pleasing company. It was the best day I've had for as long as I can remember."

She was flattered; that meant he preferred her company over Zelda's, which made her happy. *"Denke.* I had a nice time too."

He leaned forward. "How about we do this again sometime? Next time I won't look at land or do any business type stuff. It'll be just the two of us doing something …"

"Something fun?"

He chuckled. "If you like. I'll think of something. Can I see you again next Saturday?"

On Saturdays she normally worked on the farm, but Magda would urge her to accept his offer. Besides, she wanted to see him again. Being with him had given her a good rest from the daily pressures of life. "I'd like that."

"Me too. I'll walk you to the door."

CHAPTER 12

FOR THE NEXT FEW WEEKS, Jeanie and Amos saw each other every single Saturday. Mostly they stayed at his place and picnicked on the riverbank with Jasper running around. On his land, they were away from prying eyes and judgemental stares. It was so close to Malachi's death and not everyone would've approved of the budding relationship.

IT HAD ALSO BECOME a habit that Magda woke Jeanie of a morning.

Jeanie sat up as Magda handed her a tray of breakfast. *"Denke.* This looks good. I don't know what's wrong with me. I'm so tired all the time."

Her mother-in-law stared into her face. "You're not pregnant, are you?"

"Nee, I've not had morning sickness."

"Not everyone does."

Jeanie counted back months and weeks, the time since Malachi's death. It was possible, but unlikely since she'd been married for years and she had never gotten pregnant, not once. "I'm not."

"Are you sure?"

"Mm-hmm. Quite sure. Most likely I just need a tonic or something. I think I'm a little run down."

Her mother-in-law sat down on the bed beside her. "Me too. I'll take some of that tonic when you get it. I'm feeling the same. Although, I've felt like this every day for years."

Jeanie giggled. "We're a great pair you and I. Just as well Werner has a lot of energy right now to make up for us. No one ever had the energy of Malachi. He was the fullest of life person I've ever known."

As her mother-in-law talked about her sons, all Jeanie could think about was if she might be pregnant. Could it be possible after five childless years of marriage?

LATE THAT AFTERNOON, Jeanie slipped away from the fields and called the community midwife from the phone in the barn and asked her to come see her the following afternoon. She knew her mother-in-law would be out at a quilting bee and Werner would think nothing of a visitor stopping by. She would not get her hopes up. The chance of her being pregnant with her late husband's child was slim.

JEANIE STARED AT SANDRA, the community's midwife, after she'd told her of her symptoms, trying to read the expression on her face. "So, what do you think?"

"There's one sure way to know." She reached into her bag and pulled out a plastic packet. Then she ripped it open. "Pee on this."

Jeanie grimaced and took the stick from her. "Is that the only way to know?"

"There are other ways but at the early stage this is over ninety nine percent accurate. After this section's fully wet, leave it for three minutes and if the two pink lines cross you're pregnant. If only one line remains you're not."

Jeanie nodded and walked through to the bathroom.

"I'll be waiting right outside. Tell me when you've done it and I'll set my stopwatch for three minutes."

Jeanie did what she had been told to do, which

she found quite difficult because she was so nervous. Then she stared at the stick. "Okay, start the timer."

"It's on."

She closed her eyes and more than anything she wanted the test to be positive. It would be sad that the child arrived after Malachi had gone, but she would have his child and that would ease the pain of losing him. A child would brighten up all their lives.

"Okay, what does it say now?"

Jeanie looked at the stick and screamed, causing the midwife to open the door.

"You're pregnant?"

"*Jah.* Look." Jeanie held out the stick. "I am, aren't I?"

"You are." The two women hugged each other and Jeanie couldn't stop jumping around for joy.

"I can't believe it. Is it real? Could this be wrong?"

"The test? Highly unlikely."

"I can't wait to tell everyone. No, wait. I won't just now. You'll keep it quiet, won't you?"

"That's part of the job. I won't say anything to anyone ever. The news of this has come from you."

She hugged Sandra again and then picked up the stick. "*Denke,* Sandra. I'm going to be a *Mamm* at last.

I never thought this would happen. Someone will call me *Mamm*." Tears streamed down her face. "I never thought I'd hold my own *boppli* in my arms. I'll have Malachi's child to love."

Sandra put an arm around her. "You've been blessed. *Gott* has sent you comfort after the tragedy."

"*Jah. Jah,* He has." After a moment, Jeanie asked, "What happens now?"

Together they worked out how far along Jeanie was. "Nothing for a few weeks. I'll check on you every month until you're around five months and then I'll see you more often."

After Sandra left, Jeanie went out into the fields and did a few hours work before Magda came home. Just as Jeanie was preparing the evening meal, Magda came home. Jeanie looked out the kitchen window and saw Werner taking over looking after the horse and then Magda headed to the house. She couldn't wait to tell her the news.

When Magda walked into the kitchen, Jeanie said, "Sit down. I have news for you."

"I have news too."

Jeanie laughed. "Mine's more important."

"So's mine," Magda said.

"Tell me yours first then."

Magda shook her head. "Go on. Tell me yours."

Jeanie inhaled a quick breath as her heart pitter-pattered with excitement. "Well, I had Sandra here today."

Magda's eyebrows rose as she looked around. "I would've cleaned up better before I left if I'd known you were having visitors. The *haus*-work has been let go since Malachi's not been here."

"Who cares about the *haus?* It's fine anyway." Jeanie stared at her mother-in-law waiting for her to guess why Sandra was there. "You do know what Sandra does, don't you?"

"Jah, she makes quilts and we get a lot of money at auction time for them. She's got such a good eye for colors and design. *Gott* has given her a gift."

When Magda finally sat down, Jeanie pulled out the chair beside her and sat. "And what else does she do?"

"She's the midwife."

She stared at Magda.

"Why are you smiling like that?"

"Magda, I can't believe you." Jeanie shook her head.

"What have I done?" Magda put a hand to her mouth looking confused as though she'd forgotten something.

"Take a guess why the midwife would be here to see me. Why would I have called her to see me?"

Magda's jaw dropped open and her eyes bugged. "You're not!"

CHAPTER 13

JEANIE NODDED. "I am. According to her and the little stick thing. Ninety-nine point nine percent sure."

Magda squealed and then laughed. "This is the best news I've ever had in my life. I'm finally going to be a *grossmammi*. Didn't I ask you, didn't I ask you whether you were?"

"You did. You were right."

Magda grabbed Jeanie's face, placed her hands on her cheeks and kissed her forehead. *"Denke,* Jeanie. That's what I've been waiting for. I thought it'd never happen."

"Me too. It's such a shock. That explains why I've been so tired, I guess."

"And grumpy," Magda said.

Jeanie looked into Magda's green eyes. "Have I?"

"Jah. I just thought it was grief."

"Must be hormones. I had no idea I was like that."

"Nee. I was only joking." Magda giggled like a young girl.

It made Jeanie even happier to see Magda so delighted.

Then Magda stopped smiling. "You can't let him know."

"Werner?"

"Nee. You can't let Amos know."

"Well, he's going to find out sooner or later. I can't keep a secret like this for too long."

Magda stared at her and slowly shook her head. "I heard something."

"What is it?"

"He's been fooling you as much as you have him."

Jeanie frowned trying to figure out what she was talking about. "How so?"

"Amos has got someone interested in buying the farm and he's been using us to keep it nice until the sale goes through."

"What? *Nee.* It can't be true. He wouldn't. No one's come to look over the farm."

"I'm sure of it. That's what my news was. I must say, I like your news better."

"Has a sale gone through?" Jeanie thought back over the last few Saturdays she'd spent with Amos. He'd not mentioned a thing.

"*Nee,* I said someone is *interested* in it. I heard it at the quilting bee. Someone knows someone who knew someone else who was talking about buying our farm."

"I can't believe it. He's been using me?" At first, she was horrified and then all she could do was laugh. She laughed at herself for being so resistant to Amos and then for being so lonely she wanted more of Amos's company. She could see the humorous side of what was happening in her life. It wasn't long, though, before her laughter turned into tears. Their dream was going to be lost and there was nothing she could do about it. Then there was the child whom Malachi would never see. With the baby coming, the farm was more important than ever.

Magda leaned forward again and encircled her arms about her. "I'm sorry."

"Me too," she managed to say through tears.

"I never should've talked you into this thing with Amos. It was a good idea, though, wasn't it? I thought your problems would vanish if you married him. I wanted you to have what you should've had."

Jeanie wiped her eyes with the back of her hand.

"It was a terrible idea but it was my fault for agreeing. I was doing it for you and for Werner."

"What shall we do now?"

Now, Jeanie wanted Amos to fall in love with her. Not because she loved him but as a way of getting back at him. No one messed with her and got away with it. She stared at Magda. "Amos will ask me to marry him if that's the last thing I do on this earth. That man will fall in love with me and then he'll do anything I say."

Magda pressed her lips together. "Never make a decision in anger."

"Anger is all I have left."

"You have to think of the *boppli*."

"That's who I'm thinking about."

"Are you doing this because you want your *boppli* to have a *vadder*?"

"The baby has a father."

"I know that. That's not what I meant. Amos is the ideal match for you. History's repeated itself. I was in love with my first husband, and not the second. Mind you, I grew into a kind of a love for him. Now it's happening to you."

Jeanie closed her eyes and covered her face with her hands. Could she bring a baby into the world alone? Malachi would never hold his baby, never see his child grow. Tears streamed down her face. "Why now, Magda? Why couldn't I have had this *boppli* when we first got married?"

Magda pulled Jeanie's hands away from her face. "Because that's not *Gott's* timing. All things under the sun have the right time. Now is your time. *Gott* has blessed you. Don't go thinking otherwise."

"You're right. I'm pleased, I am. I know this is a miracle and I shouldn't look upon it as being anything else. I've longed for my own child for ages. It's been agony watching women get married and then having *kinner* less than a year later. I've tried so hard not to be jealous when I see pregnant women or young mothers with their *kinner*. I've always felt like such a failure. Malachi kept telling me to relax and it would happen and now it has. He was right."

"When will you let everyone know?"

"Magda, you know I can't."

Magda's eyes sparkled. "That's what I was hoping you'd say."

"Now that I'm pregnant, keeping the farm is even more vital. That's what Malachi would've wanted. We must get the farm for him, Magda, we must."

"But, at what cost?"

Jeanie wiped her eyes. "Anything it takes."

"Your child is going to need a *vadder* and if you can convince Amos to marry you, all the better."

"I don't want to have to convince anyone."

Magda put her elbows onto the table. "That's not what I meant, exactly, but if he happens to fall in love with you …"

"Do you think there's a chance the rumor you heard today could be wrong?"

"There's a chance, but I believe it's true."

"We have to hope they're wrong. I have to find out."

"What are you going to do?"

Jeanie stood and grabbed her coat from the peg by the back door. "I'm going to visit him. And, Magda don't forget, we have to keep news of my pregnancy secret from Werner. I don't want him to have the burden of being quiet about it."

"Okay. I won't say a thing."

"Good."

"I'll help you hitch the buggy. You have to be careful with yourself."

"I feel fine."

Magda stood up. "*Jah*, but all the same, you're carrying my grandchild."

Jeanie giggled. "You're such a worrier."

"You'll be the same once you have a child."

Both women walked outside to get the buggy ready.

Once Jeanie was alone in her buggy and out on the open road, she thought more about what she'd say to Amos. She had no idea and nothing came to her. She closed her eyes for a moment and enjoyed the cold fresh air on her skin. Her usual way was to face problems head on. That wouldn't work this time. She had to be strategic just in case Amos was being that way too. If Amos really had a buyer for the farm, she'd find out somehow. Then her mind raced wondering who the buyer was; whether it was someone she knew or whether there was no one at all.

CHAPTER 14

DRIVING THE BUGGY, Jeanie let out a sigh. She wanted to scream and would've done so if she'd had more energy. She had thought all her problems were solved when Zelda left. Now the problems were twice as bad. Looking down, she placed her hand over her belly. "I can't wait until you're born. I've so many things to teach you about life. I'm not being a good example right now, but this will pass and then I'll behave like a proper *mudder* and show you how to be a good young man or young lady. You won't have your *Dat,* but you'll have a nice *onkel,* and the best *grossmammi* ever."

Before she knew it, she was pulling into Amos's driveway and she still didn't know what she was going to say.

He came toward her with a worried face.

"What's wrong?" she asked.

"It's Zelda, she's coming back and she doesn't know about … She didn't ask if …"

Jeanie's heart sank. "Oh, that's not good."

"I'll tell her when she gets here."

Jeanie knew he meant that he'd tell Zelda that they'd been spending time together. "Why didn't you tell her before she left to come here?"

"I couldn't. She was already here, at the train station."

"What will you do?"

"I'll tell her that you and I …"

"Oh, Amos, we don't really know what you and I are doing." For all her anger and plotting, she couldn't stand between Amos and Zelda if they were truly meant to be together. The question loomed of whether he'd want her if he knew she was having Malachi's child.

He raised his dark eyebrows. "I hope we both feel the same. I've never had these feelings for anyone. What I have with you …" He gulped. "I feel, it's different from anything I've ever felt."

Those words were what she wanted to hear and the farm left her mind completely. "Really?"

"I wouldn't lie to you."

She took a step closer. "I've heard some things."

"What do you mean? Things about what?"

"That you have a buyer for the farm and you're making us work hard and then you'll sell it out from under us."

His eyes grew wide. "Who said such things?"

"I'm not sure. It was second, and maybe third hand information, but sometimes there's truth in those kinds of things."

"Is that what you think of me, Jeanie?"

She swallowed hard. "I don't want to think that, but you didn't give us the farm and it would've been Malachi's if only he'd gone and signed for it when you told him the paperwork was ready."

"We've been over and over this so many times, Jeanie. We're never going to agree on it."

She sensed his annoyance. "Things will have to change between us now that Zelda is back."

"*Nee.* I'll tell Zelda the truth as soon as she arrives," he said.

"Where's she staying? I heard someone's already moved into the *haus* where she was living."

"She said she's been invited to stay with Bishop Luke and Ruth."

Jeanie hoped Zelda's return wouldn't awaken old feelings within him. "I should go."

"Don't. Stay with me. She won't be here for some time."

"Okay."

They walked to the porch and he pulled a chair closer for her to sit. Once they were both seated, he said, "I have a confession to make." She held her breath. "I haven't been entirely straightforward with you."

"Go on."

"In the beginning, I didn't give the farm to you because I wanted to see more of you and that was the only contact I had with you. I didn't want you to watch potatoes grow without thinking of me."

She rubbed the side of her face as she listened. "This is surprising to hear."

"I had feelings for you before you chose Malachi, and yet I was glad for him to have you as his *fraa*. I never thought he'd have misfortune in his life and leave you a widow, but it's happened. I knew I couldn't move too quickly, but neither did I want to let you slip from my life a second time."

That confirmed his feelings for her were real. She was the one being deceiving. A tear escaped her eye and she looked away from him.

"Why have I upset you?"

"It's not you. It's just that I'm so mixed up. All I could think about was the farm and what we'd lose if we didn't have it. We all worked so hard."

"I hope the farm's not all you're thinking about these days?"

"Zelda is …"

"Zelda has nothing to do with us."

"But she's coming back here because she likes you. To take up where things left off." Things weren't adding up. If he didn't have feelings for Zelda, what was the talk about Zelda's brothers taking over?

He sighed. "I met her and we got along. Two months later, she shows up here thinking we're boyfriend and girlfriend. She even rented that house before I knew about it."

"Weren't you in a relationship?"

"I was forced into it before I knew what was happening. I never asked her to come here."

"But you wanted her brothers to take over the farm?"

"She wanted them to move here. I felt obligated and didn't know where things were going in my life. I don't want to be single and alone forever, Jeanie."

She nodded and looked up at the fluffy clouds gently floating along with the breeze. "I can understand that."

"If Malachi hadn't died, I might've ended up marrying her. Who knows?"

"I don't want to get in your way, or in Zelda's way." She felt sorry for Zelda coming back all that way thinking he'd be happy to see her.

"You've brightened my life and given —"

"Don't say any more, Amos."

He chuckled. "Why not? Don't you want to hear how I've come to care for you? I thought my chance was lost many years ago."

She bit her lip. Now she had to tell him about the baby. It wasn't fair to keep it from him now that she knew his intentions were only good. He once said that she'd have no problem finding another husband because she had no *kinner*. That could only mean one thing. He didn't want to raise another man's child. If he could have a chance with Zelda, she didn't want to ruin that for him or for her.

"There's something I must tell you."

"It's okay. I know you'll never love me like you did Malachi and I'm okay with that."

Then they heard a car. "Here she is. She's early. I don't know how she got here so fast."

Jeanie jumped to her feet and then got a little dizzy and had to sit back down. "This isn't good that she sees me here. We'll have to say we were discussing business."

He frowned at her. "I'll say nothing of the kind. She must know the truth."

"Are you sure of your feelings?" There was no time to tell him about the *boppli* now. Not with Zelda breathing down their necks.

THE AMISH POTATO FARMER'S WIDOW

"I am."

"But I need to tell you something."

"Why don't you go home? I'll stop by later and then we can talk about anything you want."

Zelda got out of the taxi and stared over at the two of them. Amos left the porch and walked over to her and Jeanie followed close behind. She'd say hello and goodbye, and then get out of there as fast as she could. She could tell by Zelda's pained expression that she didn't approve of Jeanie being at Amos's home.

CHAPTER 15

"HELLO, Zelda, it's nice to see you back. I was just leaving."

"I didn't expect to see you here, Jeanie."

"We'll talk about why she was here soon," Amos said.

Jeanie gave Zelda a little nod and then walked quickly to her buggy. All the way home, Jeanie was plagued with guilt. She shouldn't have left there without telling Amos she was pregnant. He might've felt different about his options if he'd known that. Rain started falling hard. The sky had gone from blue to gray in a matter of minutes.

WHEN JEANIE GOT HOME, Werner was there to

unhitch the buggy for her. She pulled a raincoat over her head and hurried into the kitchen to find Magda.

"You're all wet, Jeanie."

"That's because it's raining." Jeanie arranged the raincoat over a chair near the kitchen stove to dry.

Magda turned to look out the window. "So it is. I was so busy baking I didn't notice. The last time I looked out the window, the sun was shining."

"It smells amazing and I'm so hungry."

"Want some warm bread?"

"Soon, but first I have to tell you what happened."

Magda stared at her. "You talked to him?"

"*Jah,* sit down and I'll tell you."

Magda bustled over to take a seat and then Jeanie told her what had just happened with Amos, and about Zelda coming back.

"That's no good." Magda sighed and then shook her head.

"I know, I should've told him about the *boppli.* He might not be so keen on me."

"Nonsense."

"It's true, he said something about it once."

Magda locked eyes with her. "You must've misunderstood him."

Jeanie knew what she'd heard, but Magda could be so dogmatic about things sometimes it was easier not to argue. "Anyway, that aside, now that Zelda's back this might change things."

"*Nee,* you just told me he was going to tell her things wouldn't work out between them. He's been enjoying spending time with you each Saturday."

Jeanie bit her lip. "Should I go back now and tell him about the *boppli?*"

Magda's cheeks puffed. "Do we have ownership of the farm?"

"You know we don't."

"Then, *nee,* now is not the right time to tell him. Not if you don't think he'll be pleased."

Jeanie stared at her mother-in-law. She was certain being deceptive was not the right thing to do as a woman of *Gott.* It certainly didn't feel right. "He could change his mind once he sees Zelda again. I'll be forgotten."

"Don't say it."

"What's going on?" Werner said wiping his wet face with a towel.

They both turned to look at him. "You'll catch your death. Change out of those wet clothes," his mother ordered.

"I will, soon as you tell me what you were talking about."

"Nothing," Jeanie said.

"It's women's business." When he stood there

staring, Magda added, "Cramps and such." A look of horror covered Werner's face and he turned on his heel and left them alone. Magda chuckled. "Always works."

Jeanie shook her head, and then whispered, "I don't know if I can carry on with all this deception with Amos."

"Don't you want your *boppli* to call someone *Dat?*"

"I am growing fond of Amos, but Malachi has just died. I can't replace him with the snap of my fingers."

"You'll never replace Malachi. Don't even think that way."

Jeanie shrugged. "If it's meant to be, it'll happen over time someday."

"I'm an old lady and I need to tell you that things happen when you make them happen. There were two of us young women interested in Malachi's father, but I made sure he chose me."

Seeing the wicked gleam in Magda's eyes, Jeanie knew she didn't want to know any more about that. "I prefer to leave things up to *Gott*. Maybe He wants us to start somewhere else on our own, just the three of us. Well, the four of us now."

Magda shook her head. "You can't give up so easily. Amos will make a perfect husband for you.

Who else would you marry? I can't think of anyone more suitable."

Jeanie put her hand over her stomach. "I've got other things to occupy my time at the moment. And, anyway, he won't think much of me when he learns I've been deceiving him."

Swiping a hand through the air, Magda said, "Many women don't know they're pregnant until they're six or seven months along."

"That doesn't sound right. 'Many?'"

"It's true. Well, some women, anyway. Believe me."

"I can't keep secrets. If I marry him or anyone else, I have to tell them the truth. Secrets aren't good to keep." Jeanie leaned back in her chair. "I just wish we knew one way or the other. I'm past caring about the farm now. If we're going through these struggles I'm sure it's not meant to be."

"How can you say that? You're being undecided. *Gott* doesn't like lukewarm people — people who are wishy-washy. First you want the farm and then you don't. You have to make up your mind what you want. Look how hard you and Malachi have worked. Do you remember what it was like here when we arrived, and what this very *haus* was like?"

Jeanie thought back to the dusty barren fields and the house with the doors falling off the hinges, the mice dirt on the floor and even on the kitchen countertops. They'd practically rebuilt the house, too. "You're right. We put all we had into it, but Amos did say he'd get us another house. Which, I guess, kind of sounds like we're taking a handout and I don't like the way that feels." Jeanie leaned forward placing her elbows onto the table. "We have to leave this with *Gott*, Magda."

Magda lifted up her hands. *"Gott* works through these, and He uses this."* She tapped the side of her head with one of her fingers.

Jeanie kept silent. There was no point trying to reason with her mother-in-law when she set her mind on something.

THAT NIGHT, Jeanie prepared the evening meal while Magda slept. Magda often had an afternoon nap, but today she slept longer than usual.

Just when Jeanie was fixing Magda's dinner on a tray to take up to her, there was a knock on the door. She put the meal back in the oven and hurried to the door. When she opened it, she was taken aback to see three police officers. "Oh," she said with a lurch of her heart. "Hello?"

"Mrs. Yoder?"

"There are two Mrs. Yoders here. Myself and my mother-in-law."

"Were you married to Malachi Yoder?"

"Yes."

"I'm Detective Graeme." He nodded his head at the male and the female uniformed officers with him. "Officer Peters and Officer Wickers. Do you mind if we come in?"

She stepped back. "Yes. I mean, no. I don't mind. Come in." She showed them to the living room, still flustered, wondering what was wrong. Were they going to say that Malachi was in the wrong and the accident had been his fault?

"We're sorry to have to tell you this, but we have reason to believe your husband's death was no accident."

CHAPTER 16

JEANIE GASPED AT THE NEWS. If her husband's death hadn't been an accident, did they mean that he'd been murdered? She looked at the three strangers and tried to figure out what they meant. "What?"

"I'm afraid it's so." Detective Graeme nodded and the corners of his mouth downturned.

"He was murdered?"

The detective said, "The driver of the car, who is now deceased, was a known criminal. In his possession, we found a note with instructions on how to hit a buggy so the occupant, your husband, would be thrown out."

She gasped again. "No!"

He nodded. "We have reason to believe he was paid to kill your husband or at least cause him serious injury. It's obvious he wasn't planning on killing himself in the process."

Werner came into the room and when he saw Jeanie's distressed face he rushed to sit beside her and put his arm around her. "What's going on?"

Jeanie said, "This is my husband's brother."

The detective repeated what Jeanie had been told. "Do you know anyone who'd have wanted to harm your husband in any way, Mrs. Yoder?"

Jeanie looked at Werner, and he shook his head. "No," he said, looking at Detective Graeme.

"Me either," Jeanie said. "I can't believe this. I thought it was just an accident."

Werner said, "What do you know about this man, the driver of the car?"

"Mitchell Booker was a criminal for hire. He'd do anything for a price. He'd been arrested for armed robbery and several incidents of breaking and entering over the years."

"Tell me about Malachi," the detective said.

Jeanie looked at him. "He was a good man."

"He worked on the farm here?"

"Yes, he did. We all work on it," Jeanie said.

Detective Graeme leaned forward looking between Jeanie and Werner. "Who inherits the farm?"

Jeanie and Werner looked at one another. She

looked back at Graeme "We don't own it," Jeanie told him.

"Who's the owner?" Detective Graeme pulled out a pen and a notebook.

"Amos Troyer. He's from our community."

"And how would we contact Amos Troyer?"

"I can give you his address," Werner said.

"Go on."

While Werner gave him Amos's address, Jeanie's thoughts turned to Magda. How would she tell her this awful news? "No one would want to kill Malachi," Jeanie said.

"It's still under investigation, but it does appear your husband's death was no accident. Otherwise, we certainly wouldn't be disturbing you like this."

Tears escaped her eyes. "I can't believe it." She stood up and wanted only to be by herself.

Werner jumped to his feet. "I think you should leave us alone now if that's all right?"

"Yes, of course." The three of them stood. "We'll be in touch." Detective Graeme handed over a card. "Here's my number. If you think of anything that might help our investigation, please call us."

"Thank you." Werner took the card. "We will." As Werner showed them out, Jeanie collapsed onto the couch and everything faded around her.

Jeanie opened her eyes to see two worried faces;

Werner and Magda were leaning over her. Confused, she tried to sit up and Magda said, "Wait. Stay there. Werner, get her some water." Werner disappeared, and Magda said, "You fainted."

Jeanie wondered if she'd been dreaming. She looked around. "The police?"

"They're gone. Werner told me what they said."

Jeanie closed her eyes. It was true. It made everything worse. There were so many things she didn't understand. She had naively thought, back when she joined the community and gave her life over to God, all her troubles and worries would disappear and she'd have a life of safety and peace. Then Malachi died … no, he was killed. Was God testing her? That had to be it.

Was it God's will Malachi had been murdered, or was it some evil force that had cut short his life? She felt a wet cloth on her forehead and opened her eyes. Werner had come back with a glass of water and Magda was arranging the cool washcloth. Relaxing, she was grateful for their loving care.

"Sit up and have a drink," Magda said after a few minutes.

She took the cloth from her forehead, gave it to Magda, and sat up. After a sip of water, she looked at Magda. "Werner told you?"

"*Jah.*"

Jeanie knew they were trying not to worry her by keeping quiet about it. "Who would've done it and why?"

"It's not for us to concern ourselves with, Jeanie. Vengeance belongs to *Gott*. He will punish the person who did this to Malachi."

"That's right. You have to put it out of your mind," Werner said, and then added, *"Mamm* told me about the *boppli."*

"Magda! I thought we were keeping it quiet."

"You've gotta tell me. I'm family," Werner said. "I'm an *onkel."*

"I told Werner and that's all. He knows to keep it quiet. He won't say anything. I was worried when you fainted."

Jeanie took another sip of water wondering who would want her husband dead. "He never harmed anyone. He only ever helped people."

"Don't be concerned about that now. It must've been a mistake. Police don't know everything."

Jeanie nodded, but in her heart, she knew there was no error. Malachi's name was on that piece of paper from the other man's car. She was certain that's what the police had said. Tomorrow, she would visit the police and find out all she could.

CHAPTER 17

JEANIE KNEW Magda would disapprove of her going to the police, so she'd had to let her think she was going to run some errands. As soon as she walked into the police station, she saw Detective Graeme talking with someone. When he saw her, he excused himself and walked over.

"Mrs. Yoder. You've remembered something?"

"I'd like to ask some more questions if I could."

"Yes. Come through to an interview room."

Once they sat, the detective began, "I've just been talking to Amos Troyer. It's interesting to us that the owner of the farm you're living on knew the deceased."

"Of course, he did. They grew up together." She frowned at the detective. "Of course Amos would know who was living on his farm."

"No, sorry. I'm not talking about your husband, Mrs. Yoder. I'm referring to Mitchell Booker, the driver of the car."

"Amos knew the driver? The man who crashed into my husband's buggy?"

The detective nodded.

Jeanie wondered how Amos would know an *Englischer* who was also a criminal. "How did he know him, did he say?"

"No, he didn't, but one or two of Booker's acquaintances said an Amish man had been talking to him."

"Where was he talking to him?"

"At a club."

Jeanie shook her head. "Amos would never go near a club. Most definitely not."

The detective raised his graying bushy eyebrows. "We have CCTV footage telling us otherwise."

"Can I see it?" She was convinced it wasn't Amos.

"No. It's in evidence. We might need you to view it later, though."

"I doubt it's him. It wouldn't be. Was the man in Amish clothes?"

"Yes."

"It could easily be someone else then. It could've been anyone. Was there a clear view of his face?"

He stared at her and she was sure there was pity in his eyes. "How can I help you today, Mrs. Yoder?"

She swallowed hard ignoring the uneasiness within. "I want to learn more about this man you say killed my husband."

"There's not much to know. If you wait a moment, I'll get the file."

"Sure." While he was gone, she looked around the gray room. There was a camera in one corner of the room, but no mirrors like she'd seen on police shows she'd watched before she'd joined the community. From how Detective Graeme had been talking, it seemed Amos was the only suspect.

When Graeme got back, he sat down and opened the folder, pulled out a mug shot and slid it across the table to her. "This is Booker. Have you seen him before?"

The man in the photo had short dark hair and a large moustache. His eyes were close together, a classic trait of criminals in the mystery books she used to read in her former life. "No. I don't believe I have."

He took the photo back. "As I told you, he's been in and out of trouble most of his life. Since he was sixteen, and probably even younger."

"Do you have any idea why this man would've done this?"

"Money. Someone paid him. The question we need answered is, who would want your husband out of the way?"

"I can't think of anyone. Malachi was just a quiet man who worked hard on our farm. He got along with everyone and didn't associate with anyone from outside our community."

"Are you certain of that?"

"Yes. He wouldn't have had the time even if he'd wanted to."

The detective moved in his chair. "What happens now that he's gone?"

"In what way?" she asked.

"For a start, what happens to the potato farming business?"

"I'm not certain." She didn't like to tell him all the carrying on that had happened with Amos.

He leaned forward. "What do you mean?"

"Well … haven't you talked with Amos Troyer?"

"Yes, but I'm interested in your version of things."

She frowned at the detective. "We're staying on for another few months and then Amos will decide what he's doing with the farm." She didn't tell the detective about Amos offering them a house because that might look as though Amos wanted them off the farm urgently.

"What are the financial arrangements with Mr. Troyer? Are you leasing the farm from him?"

Frowning, she asked, "Surely you don't need to know all this?"

"It might help."

"Look, I converted to Amish and I know they do things very differently. You might not understand how they do business. It's all about relationships and it's not about the money. They do handshake agreements on most things."

The detective laughed. "Everything's about money and I'm sure the Amish are no different."

"You're wrong."

"I don't believe so. Either way, tell me about the arrangement with Troyer."

She sat there and told him the truth of how they came to run the farm and had built it up from nothing. "So, you see, it would benefit Amos to keep us there."

"But why would he want you to stay now that it's valuable? Couldn't he sell it? According to my information, when he inherited the farm it was run down. I'd say Troyer has done very well out of your family."

"And, so have we. We got to keep all the entire profits."

"Hmm. Which I'm guessing were next to nothing

in the first years. You see, I was raised on a farm not too far from here."

"We got by. We don't need much."

"What's to stop Amos from selling it from underneath you?"

"He wouldn't. Well, he might." Magda had told her she heard that Amos had a buyer. She could see the detective's mind ticking over. "If you're thinking Amos had anything to do with my husband's death, you're barking up the wrong tree."

"We have to follow every lead. We look at those closest to the deceased and work our way out. Take you for example."

Jeanie flew to her feet and pointed her finger at him. "Don't you dare say I might have employed that man to kill my husband."

"Calm down, Mrs. Yoder. That's not what I'm thinking."

She sat back down rubbing her face. Her anger had flared again. When she composed herself, she looked up at the detective. "I apologize. Just find the person who did it."

"That's what we're doing."

Tears fell down her face and she covered her mouth. "What do you need me to do?"

"Go home. Go home and pray for us to find the people who did this to your husband."

Jeanie nodded. "I can do that."

"Will you be okay?"

She wiped her eyes. "Yes."

ON WOBBLY LEGS, Jeanie walked out of the police station. When she saw a nearby bus-stop seat, she sat down. Her buggy was parked a distance around the corner and she needed to rest a moment. She knew her eyes must've been red and she avoided looking at people who walked by.

The only thing she could do was keep her mind on positive things. What did the farm matter? She was soon to welcome her child into the world. Whether her husband was murdered or whether his death was an accident, he was still gone and there was nothing that could change that. After giving herself a stern talking to and willing herself to carry on, she stood and walked to her waiting buggy.

On the way back to the farm, she drove past Amos's house and was surprised to see Zelda's buggy there. It struck her as odd. Surely Amos told her that things wouldn't work out between them and then she would've gone back home. It was just another worry to add to her ever-increasing list of things to try not to worry about.

When she got home, Magda came outside. "Where have you been?" she called out.

"I went to the police station."

Magda walked closer. "Why didn't you take me with you?"

"I don't know. I wanted to save you the stress, I guess."

"What did they say?"

"Nothing much. I talked with Detective Graeme. They're still investigating and haven't learned anything new." She walked closer so Werner wouldn't hear. "They asked questions about Amos. I think they are looking at him as a possible suspect."

"That's ridiculous."

"I know, but that's what they told me. They think he'll profit with Malachi out of the way, and they said Amos knew the man who died in that car. They said they had him — Amos, I mean — at a club talking to him on CCTV footage. They think he paid that man to hit Malachi's buggy."

"Is that so?"

"*Jah,* but it could've been any Amish man on that footage. They all look the same in their clothes, don't they?"

"That's right. It doesn't sound like something Amos would do. Did you tell them that Amos offered Malachi the farm and had drawn papers up to give it to him?"

"*Nee.* I didn't. Maybe I did leave that part out. I told him everything else about the arrangement Malachi had with Amos. Detective Graeme thinks Amos has a buyer for the farm, just like you heard."

Magda looked out over the fields. "I don't know if it'll be profitable this year."

"Most likely not, but still it's better than the barren earth we found when we got here, and I've got last year's figures to prove it."

Magda shook her head. "You shouldn't go anywhere by yourself. You could've fainted again. Take me with you from now on. Okay?"

"I will."

Magda stepped forward. "You mean it?"

"I do."

"I've made soup for lunch. You need to keep your strength up. I'll have Werner handle the horse and buggy." After Magda had yelled for her son to come back from the fields, Magda and Jeanie walked inside.

JEANIE SAT QUIETLY with her mother-in-law as they ate their chicken and corn chowder. "I don't think Amos has a buyer."

"That's what I heard," Magda said.

"He's straightforward with things. He told me about Zelda's brothers and if he had a buyer I'm sure he would've said so."

"You might be right. Time will tell."

Jeanie gazed upon her creamy soup. "Time is something we don't have a lot of."

CHAPTER 18

WHEN SATURDAY ROLLED AROUND, Jeanie asked Magda to meet Amos's buggy at their regular time of nine in the morning when he arrived at the farm. Magda told Amos Jeanie wasn't feeling very well. He sent his regards and went home.

Jeanie hoped she was doing the right thing, but if she spent any more time alone with him she'd have to tell him about the baby. They never talked to one another much at the meetings on Sundays in case they set tongues wagging. Through the week, they both worked, so Saturdays were all they had.

On Saturday afternoon, Magda and Jeanie once again worried about their future as they made a large evening meal, enough so there'd be leftovers for their day of rest.

"I should be relaxing and looking forward to my

baby rather than worrying about everything." Jeanie continued to chop carrots into small pieces.

"You can relax when this is all over."

"But, what will the police reveal and who could've wanted Malachi dead? There must be some mistake."

"What if Amos wanted him gone?" Magda said.

"What are you saying?"

"Well, it's possible it's his way of getting you and the farm, Jeanie."

Jeanie narrowed her eyes at her. "Don't joke about it."

"I'm sorry. You've been spending time with him, so maybe he'll changed his mind about selling. Just like he changed his mind about Zelda, and also Zelda's brothers. That only proves what I said. He liked you a long time ago."

"Let's rethink what we believe to be true. Who would profit from Malachi being injured? Zelda, so she could have her brothers help run the farm and eventually take it over?"

Magda shook her head.

"Why not? What do we know about her?" Jeanie asked.

"Enough to know she's not a murderer. It must've been an *Englischer* who did it." Magda filled a pot with water and then set it on the lit stovetop.

"Why don't we investigate things ourselves?"

Magda sat back down. "How?"

"We'll invite them here to the farm, Zelda and her brothers. What if we say we're considering leaving the farm, and we bring all the brothers here to teach them what to do?"

Magda grimaced. "That's only a good idea if we're convinced it was one of them."

"We could find out."

"How?"

Jeanie sighed. "I'm not sure. One of us would have to get closer to Zelda. She already doesn't like me." Jeanie hoped Magda would offer to befriend her.

"I think you're wrong, Jeanie. She might not like you, but she might decide to be nice to you to find out exactly what's going on between you and Amos."

"He changed his mind about the brothers but I don't know how else we can find out if it was one of them. They're the only ones I can think of who stood to gain anything with Malachi out of the way. I'll see if I can talk things over with Amos. I'll tell him the farm is getting a bit much for us."

"Then we'll have to change our course when we find out more. For now, we go with what we know."

Jeanie leaned back in her chair and held her head. She felt like she was in a family of gangsters plotting against someone. This was not the life she had thought she'd have when she joined the Amish and married Malachi.

THAT NIGHT, all Jeanie wanted was to be in a dark room, somewhere quiet, where she wouldn't have to think. "I'll have an early night if you can do my share of the washing up, Werner?" Jeanie asked.

"Of course."

"Not feeling well?" Magda asked.

"It's all a bit too much for me."

"Mind those stairs."

"I'll be careful. Don't worry." Jeanie climbed the steep stairs that they'd always planned to fix, and opened her bedroom door. She pulled off her prayer *kapp* before she went and looked out the window across the darkened fields. When Malachi was alive, they'd look out that very window most evenings, and they'd both felt a sense of pride at what they'd accomplished. Was God now punishing them for that pride? It was God who gave the increase. Had they moved their focus away from God in their diligence to make a profit and keep the farm at any cost? Was He angry with them? She covered her tummy with her hand and prayed.

Would God want them to discover who paid that

man to crash into Malachi's buggy? She moved to her bedside table, unpinned and then unbraided her nearly waist-length hair. Then she slowly ran her fingers through it to loosen the tangles as she tried to untangle her thoughts.

She was reminded that there was no security in this world except with God. For her peace of mind and the health of her baby, she had to rely on Him. Without her husband to lean on, He was now all she had.

Standing by the window again, a cold shiver rippled up her spine. She was there alone in the room that she once shared with Malachi.

There was a gaping void in her life without having someone to share it with. Magda was right, it would be better for her child to have a male figure to grow up with. Even though Werner was living with them now, he wouldn't be there forever. He'd meet some lovely girl and get married, then it would be just Magda and her alone. Two lonely widows raising a child.

She heaved a sigh, undid her apron and lifted her dress over her head. Reaching under her pillow, she took hold of her cotton nightgown and pulled it on. This place had been her home for so long it would be hard to leave it, but now it was becoming more likely every day. The only way she could cope with the future was to be carefree about the outcome. *Whatever is your will, God. Thy will be done.* She got into bed and slid under the quilt, closed her eyes and focused her thoughts on the pleasant times she'd had with Malachi.

As much as she tried, her mind kept going back to sorrow-filled places.

Never would she feel Malachi's warm breath on her neck, never enjoy the caress of his fingertips, or the softness of his lips against hers. She had no hand to hold while drifting off to sleep. Her life would be forever filled with lonely nights in cold beds. Her thoughts turned to her child, who'd never see Malachi's face and never even hear the sound of his voice.

Sleep came to Jeanie that night, but not before her pillow was soaked with her tears.

THE NEXT DAY at the Sunday meeting, Jeanie had one thing on her mind and that was what she'd say to Amos when she spoke with him. Jeanie looked over at Amos as she sat with Magda in one of the center rows waiting for the meeting to begin.

"I see Zelda's here. She didn't go home like you

thought she would," Magda leaned over and whispered in Jeanie's ear.

"I just overheard that one of Zelda's brothers is coming tomorrow and staying for a few weeks. They still want to move to this community."

Magda's eyes flickered with annoyance. "Make sure you talk with him and find out exactly what's going on."

"I will, don't worry."

They sat through the meeting and Jeanie was so churned up about her uncertain future that she barely listened to a word of the teachings. After the meeting, she waited until Amos was alone.

"How are you feeling?" he asked when she approached.

"Much better, *denke.*"

"You don't look too good."

She raised her eyebrows. "That's because I'm a little confused about something. Did you tell Zelda about us?"

"I did."

"Then what's going on with Zelda's brother coming here?"

"I feel obligated to help her brothers because I told her I would. I mentioned I can find work for them here."

Jeanie shook her head. "You mention a lot of things, Amos."

He stared at her and she could see the concern in his dark eyes. "I'm only trying to help people."

"What did you say to her?"

"Zelda?"

"Jah."

He took a deep breath. "It didn't go as well as I hoped. I told her I had feelings for someone else and she dismissed it. It was as though she didn't hear. I tried, believe me. I don't want to string her along or give her a false impression, but what can I do if she won't listen?"

"That would be hard." She shook her head. "I'm sorry, Amos. I'm just feeling out of sorts today. I'm grumpy."

He chuckled. "It's okay. I can understand that."

"There's no excuse for a bad mood."

"Your life has changed in a short space of time. It can be excused."

She shook her head. "I don't want it to keep changing."

He slowly nodded, and then they were interrupted by Zelda. "What are you two talking about?" Her attitude was fun and carefree and not at all like her usual self.

"Amos was just telling me your *bruder* is coming to stay soon."

"*Jah.* One of them. I have three. They're wanting to move here. I've told them all about this community and the opportunities here."

"That's good. I hope they move here."

"*Denke* for your kind offer, Jeanie."

"Um, what was that?" Jeanie asked.

"Magda told me just now that my *bruder* is welcome to stay at the farm, so Werner can show him how the place is run."

Jeanie opened her mouth about to say something when she saw Amos staring at her in disbelief.

"What's going on?" Amos asked Jeanie.

"It seems Magda has invited Zelda's *bruder* to stay with us for a few weeks, or however long he wants." She looked up at Zelda. Things hadn't gone according to plan, but maybe that was for the best. "When did you talk with Magda?"

"Just now."

"I've got to see someone about something. Excuse me." Jeanie left them and walked away to the other side of the bishop's yard. She looked back and saw Amos looking about for her, so she deliberately joined in a conversation with a group of people. Before long, Amos was right beside her.

"Can I have a word with you, Jeanie?"

"Sure." She took a few steps away with him.

"What are you doing? Don't you want the farm now?"

"I do. Nothing's changed."

"Then what was all that about just now? Why would you encourage Jeanie's *bruder?* It doesn't make sense."

"It was Magda who invited her. Have the police been to see you?"

"About the accident?"

"Jah."

"They have. They've questioned me on a couple of occasions, why?"

"It's just that they think it wasn't an accident."

His eyebrows drew together. "What then if it wasn't an accident?"

She looked around about her and then whispered, "They found a note at the man's place, the driver of the car. There was a note explaining where to best hit the buggy to tip it over. Where to hit it and so forth and at what speed."

"Nee."

She nodded. "It's true."

"They didn't tell me that." He rubbed his chin. "What does this have to do with having Zelda's *bruder* —"

Jeanie took a deep breath, and thought it best to

tell the truth. "Magda and I wondered if one or more of Zelda's brothers wanted Malachi out of the way, to clear the farm for them. They might not have meant to kill him, just injure him. What do you know about her brothers?"

"Don't tell me that you believe it too?"

"Well, I don't know, but the police found … Did they tell you they think you were talking to the man who died in the car? I think that they think you might have paid him to do it." She could see the horrified look on Amos's face. "The driver was a criminal and he was paid to crash into the buggy."

"I didn't do it. I'll talk to the police tomorrow and straighten this whole thing out. Why would someone want Malachi harmed?"

"I have no idea. Do you know Zelda's brothers?"

"I've never met them, but they're well-respected members of their community."

Jeanie looked over at Zelda. "Why are they so anxious to leave their community then?"

"Lack of work. Look, I don't think it's a good idea to have him stay with you. He would've had nothing to do with it. Besides, what are you going to do, torture him, interrogate him?"

"My husband was murdered and I want to find out who did it."

"What difference will it make? He's gone."

"I just need to know."

"The end result is still the same. He's not coming back."

"I know that." Her head was swimming. "I need to sit down."

"Are you okay? You're pale and you're not making a lot of sense."

She had to think fast. The last thing she wanted was for him to guess she was pregnant. "Ah, my blood pressure's been a little low."

He grabbed a nearby chair and brought it over for her to sit on. Then he took hold of another and sat beside her for a while. "I can't allow Zelda's *bruder* to stay with you."

"You don't trust us?"

"It's not that. I can't give him or Zelda false hope. I've already decided to leave the farm with you."

"You have?"

He nodded and smiled at her.

She took a deep breath. "I don't know what to say."

"I've been giving it a lot of thought. Malachi would've wanted you and his mother and brother to have the farm. I was looking at things from a purely selfish viewpoint."

She felt guilty for setting out to be nice to him, to

soften him. "We can pay you off, a little at a time and when we get a good harvest —"

"You'll do no such thing. Anyway, I've got bigger things to worry about. I'll sort things out with the police tomorrow, so I don't find myself in jail."

"They would've found out it wasn't you." Jeanie would feel better knowing who had paid that man to run into Malachi's buggy.

"Well, I'd like to make certain they know I didn't have anything to do with it. And, I will talk to Zelda and tell her it's not a good idea for her brother to stay on the potato farm."

"Thank you." It was a burden off her shoulders that Zelda's brother wouldn't be staying with them.

"I'll tell her I'm giving it to you."

"Really?"

"Jah."

"Denke so much, Amos. I can hardly believe it."

"I'll see the lawyers first thing tomorrow. Wait, I'll see the police first, and then I'll go to the lawyers. I don't like seeing you distressed like this."

Jeanie giggled. "Are you sure about this?"

"Of course I am. This is what should've happened to start with."

"I can't wait until I tell Magda. She'll be so pleased. I won't let her know just yet. I'll wait until we get home."

"If you'll excuse me, I'll have to break the news to Zelda." He walked away.

Now she had what she wanted, but she felt bad for the way she'd gone about getting it. Surely God wouldn't be pleased.

CHAPTER 19

LATER THAT NIGHT, she sat with Magda in their kitchen celebrating the good news while waiting for Werner to get home from the singing.

Their peaceful night was shattered by the crashing, tinkling sounds of breaking glass.

The two women jumped to their feet. "What was that?" Magda asked.

"The living room." Jeanie raced to the living room with Magda close behind her. The room was covered in splinters of glass. They heard a car rev its engine just as they saw the car turn on its headlights and speed away. Jeanie covered her mouth. "We could've been in here."

"Who would've done this?"

Jeanie didn't like to say it, but what if it was the same person who had wanted her husband dead?

"We know it wasn't one of Zelda's brothers. They live too far away."

"Unless they paid someone to do it."

"I don't want to think about that."

"You sit down, Jeanie. I'll clear this up."

"*Nee*. We'll do it together."

They started by carefully picking up the largest pieces. Then Jeanie spied a large rock. "Look at this." She leaned down and picked it up.

"They threw that?"

"Seems like it." It was a large rock; the person who threw it must've been strong. "There's paper wrapped around it." Jeanie carefully peeled off the paper and saw it was a note. Then she read it out. "No one leaves me." Fear rippled through her when she recognized the writing. "This is my *Englischer* ex-boyfriend's writing. Tony Hansford."

"Are you sure?"

"Yes. I'm positive. He used to leave me notes every day telling me what to do. He was an awful, awful man. I ran away from him and that's when Malachi found me. When I got that flat tire."

"I'll call the police."

"*Nee*. He might be still out there somewhere."

The two women huddled together in the kitchen until Werner came home. When he arrived, Jeanie went out and told him what had happened. He waited with her while she called the police from their phone in the barn, and then they hurried back to the house.

Detective Graeme and a team of evidence technicians arrived in two white vans within half an hour. By that time, they'd cleaned up all the broken glass.

He picked up the note with tweezers. "You say your ex-boyfriend wrote this?"

"That's right. I know his writing well."

He slipped it into a plastic sleeve. "We'll dust it for his prints." Then he took down his name and last known address.

"Do you think he was the one who …?"

"We'll find out. We're taking a cast of the tire tracks."

She saw out the window that they'd set up large lights and were leaning over doing things on the ground.

"I'd like you to come into the station tomorrow. We'll have to get your fingerprints to rule them out when we're checking the rock and the note, and I'd like you to look at the CCTV footage we have."

"Good. Because I know it's not Amos Troyer. I'd really like to see it."

"It could be someone you know."

She'd never forgive herself if her ex-boyfriend had ordered her husband murdered.

Werner was busy in the living room, putting wood over the broken window until they could get someone out to fix it.

WHEN JEANIE ARRIVED at the police station the next morning, she asked to speak with Detective Graeme and was ushered into an empty interview room. She waited alone for a few minutes until he walked in. "Good morning, Mrs. Yoder."

"Hello. Has Amos Troyer been in to see you this morning?"

"Yes. We've sorted everything out as far as he's concerned. The man we thought was him wasn't Amish at all. Troyer pointed out some things out that weren't authentic for an Amish man to wear. Someone was out to fool us."

"How could you ever have thought it was Amos Troyer?"

"Looked like him to me."

"It was a disguise, used in case cameras were on him. I'd say it was Tony who did it. He's violent and shrewd."

He pushed forward a note in a plastic sleeve; she recognized the writing. "That's Tony's handwriting for sure."

"This is the note we found in Booker's trailer."

Jeanie shook her head. "Was Tony trying to kill me or my husband? There's no name mentioned here. From what you said before, I thought my husband's name was on the paper. I was the one who normally took that drive into town every Tuesday. We started growing vegetables when we moved to the potato farm. We knew it would supplement our income, and put food on our table. I regularly drove in to the markets to collect payment for the wagonload of vegetables we delivered every Saturday morning."

"Who would've known that?"

"Anyone could've known."

"Hansford might've been watching you for some time."

"Do you think you can find him?"

A smile twitched at the corners of his lips. "We're holding him for questioning right now."

"Has he confessed?"

"Not yet, but it'll help that you've recognized his handwriting. All we have to do is tie him to the footage we've got and match his tires to the casts we took last night."

Jeanie let out the breath she'd been holding in. "I hope I don't see him when I leave here."

"We'll hold him for as long as we can. Don't worry yourself."

"I'll try not to."

"From what we know, a long-term girlfriend left him not too long ago, and it seems he wanted to get back at all the women who walked out on him."

"By hurting my husband?"

"People like him are irrational, but he could've meant Mitchell Booker to hit the buggy with you driving it. Wait right here. I'll see how far they've gotten with him."

As she waited for the detective to return, she thought back over the whole thing. She felt bad for thinking her husband's murder might have had something to do with Zelda's brothers. It'd had nothing to do with the potato farm.

When he walked back in he was smiling.

"What's happening?"

"Hansford confessed."

"Really?"

"Yes. He had a vendetta he was going to carry out. Now he sees he's beaten. For now, there's no need for you to view the CCTV footage."

"Did he hurt anyone else?"

"Not that we know of at this stage."

Jeanie shook her head. "He's not a stable man. He needs help."

"Well, let's hope he gets it, shall we? First, we'll charge him and try to keep him off the streets. He could get bail, so I'd advise you to be watchful over the next several months."

"I will."

"I'll keep you informed."

"Thank you." She stood up and offered her hand and he stood and shook it.

"Thank you for your co-operation."

As she was at the door, she turned around. "He was trying to kill me?"

"He didn't admit to that."

"Oh." She turned and walked out of the room closing the door behind her. When she got to the entranceway, she was joined by Magda who had been waiting for her. She was so glad to see her friendly face.

"What happened?" Magda asked.

"I just need to get out into the fresh air and then I'll tell you everything." It was hard to tell Malachi's mother that the man had meant to cause her harm, but she was through with being deceptive. "It was horrible, Magda. Tony was in one of those interview rooms. It was way too close and it made me feel awful."

"You didn't see him?"

"*Nee.*" She explained everything to Magda as they

walked to the buggy, and then added, "Something went wrong somewhere for the driver of the car to get killed as well."

"The man was misguided, most likely trapped in a life of crime and he died for it."

Jeanie looked over at Magda and was reminded of the reason she was attracted to God's people. They were humble and gentle people. "Tony dressed in Amish clothes while he was arranging with that man to kill me, or injure me." Jeanie shook her head. "That was so weird."

"Why would the police think he looked like Amos? Do they look alike?"

"*Nee,* not at all. Well, I suppose they have the same build but that's all."

They reached the buggy. "At least, we can relax with the farm with Amos giving it to you."

"I must tell him the truth about everything." Jeanie climbed into the buggy.

Standing outside the buggy looking in, Magda said, "Truth about what?"

"I have to tell him I tried to make him like me."

Magda got in beside her. "I don't think that's a good idea."

"It's just something I have to do." She looked behind her and moved her buggy out onto the road. "Please don't try to talk me out of it. I also need to tell him about the *boppli*." Jeanie didn't like to be a person who was swayed by the opinions of others, but that was what she'd become. Malachi had always told her to listen to her heart, and she was going to, starting from that moment.

CHAPTER 20

WHEN JEANIE HAD TAKEN her mother-in-law home, she felt she had to head over to Amos's place to make her confessions about everything. He deserved the truth. In time, she might have married a man such as Amos since she wasn't the kind of woman who liked to be alone.

As much as she loved Malachi, he was gone and she was still very much alive with, God willing, a long life ahead of her. Every mile of the journey, she thought how easy it would be to remain silent and not tell Amos of her deceit. It would be the simplest way.

She sat in the buggy when she arrived at his house, summoning the courage to face him. With a good deal of self-talk, she got out of the buggy and knocked on Amos's door. When he opened it, a smile spread across his face and then she struggled to find words to begin her confession.

"What is it?"

"I need to talk to you about something." She shook her head.

"Has something bad happened?"

She shook her head. "Well, maybe."

He led her into the house and sat her down on the couch. He sat beside her and took her hand. "Tell me what it is."

She gently took her hand away from his, not feeling worthy of his touch. "Did you go to the police today?"

She knew he'd been there.

"I did and told them all the reasons it couldn't have been me on that footage they had. For a start, I had guests staying here on that day."

"I went there shortly after you'd been there and they got the man who paid that man to kill Malachi. He was really after me, it seems."

"Your ex-boyfriend was the one who did it?"

"*Jah.*" She felt so bad that she was the indirect cause of her husband's death.

"Werner was telling me some things about it."

Now she was worried about what else Werner might have told him. "I need to come clean with you about a few things."

His eyebrows pinched together. "What?"

"I've deceived you."

His brow furrowed. "In what way?"

She wanted to tell him that she deliberately set out to make him fall in love with her but she couldn't, she just couldn't hurt him that badly. "You see, I must. I'm having a baby." Both hands instinctively flew to her belly.

His eyebrows rose. "Really?"

"*Jah.* And it's a tragic thing that Malachi will never see his child. I guess this means the end for us."

"This is just the beginning. Marry me, Jeanie, so your child can have a *vadder.*"

She shook her head. "*Denke,* but it wouldn't be right to marry just for the sake of the child."

"Marry me, then, because I love you."

She swallowed hard. "You ... you what?"

He chuckled. "I was deciding when to ask you and it might as well be now. I don't know what I've been waiting for."

She couldn't agree without another confession. All she wanted to do was run away. When she rose to her feet, she felt strange and had to sit back down.

"Be careful."

She took a moment, and then said, "I just told

you I'm pregnant and I know that's something *you* wouldn't want. You told me so once."

He drew back. "I don't believe I said any such thing."

"You did. You said that I would be attractive to men and would have no trouble marrying again because I didn't have *kinner*."

"I might've said something like that to give you encouragement. It had nothing to do with me because I didn't have strong feelings for you then, not like I do now. If you agree to marry me, I'll be the happiest man in the world that we can have a child."

She was relieved to hear that, but she still had more to say and she was leading into it. "It just wouldn't work between us."

"I don't know why you say that. We get along well."

She shook her head. "It just wouldn't."

"I love you, Jeanie, and I was under the impression you might have similar feelings for me."

Jeanie nodded. "I do, but things are complicated now."

He chuckled. "Where there is life, there will always be complications."

"That's true, but there are things you don't know about me."

He chuckled. "There's one hundred and one things we don't know about each other, but we can learn as we go."

She was still too scared to tell of her deception, so she simply said, "It's too soon after Malachi's death."

He looked down and slowly nodded. "I can understand that. I'll be here for you whenever you're ready."

Now she felt bad and guilty. "Don't wait for me." She shook her head.

"I will. You're the woman I want to share my life with. I've never felt like this about any other woman." He looked earnestly into her eyes.

"But, I don't want to stop you if you can find happiness with someone else."

"There is no happiness elsewhere. I liked you way back when you first came to the community. When I saw you at the very first meeting in your *Englischer* clothes and your worried face and wide eyes. I said to myself, *that's the woman I'm going to marry.*" He chuckled. "At that time, I had no idea it was Malachi who'd brought you to that meeting. I had no chance, then — I couldn't try to take you from my friend. But now God has given me a second chance with you. I won't lose you again. I'll wait until you're ready."

"And, if I'm never ready?"

"I will have to content myself with admiring you from afar and dreaming of the day we'll be as one."

She looked down at the floor. If only she hadn't listened to Magda. Then again, she had to take responsibility for her actions. She learned a valuable lesson out of this, but it had come at a great price. "Why does life have to be so wretched?"

"That's our lot in life, I guess, but we make the best of it. We make the most of our happy times and turn to *Gott* in times of trouble."

"I won't hold you up anymore today. I just wanted to tell you why I can't see so much of you anymore." She slowly rose to her feet and he jumped up.

"Careful."

"I'm okay."

He took hold of her hand and walked with her to the door.

CHAPTER 21

WHEN JEANIE MOVED through the doorway, Amos brought her hand to his mouth and kissed it. Her heart felt like it would break. All she wanted was to be held in his arms, but he wouldn't be acting like this if he knew of her deception. She pulled her hand back and hated herself for being such a coward. "Goodbye, Amos."

"I'll walk you to the buggy." He helped her into the buggy and then she clicked her horse forward.

When she got to the bottom of the driveway, tears threatened. They couldn't take the potato farm now. She'd have to tell Magda and Werner they'd have to leave. There was too much sadness associated with it now.

Once the baby arrived, she'd get a job somewhere or she could even do freelance bookwork from home.

Magda would look after the *boppli* while she worked. Werner could get a job somewhere and they'd all live together.

She looked back at Amos's house and saw him walking inside the front door. When she moved onto the road, she heard a car. She moved to one side to allow the car to pass since it was traveling so fast. Instead of passing, the car stopped beside her.

Glancing down, she saw it was Tony. Her heart pounded in fear.

"Get out!"

"No." Fear filled her entire body. He'd come to kill her himself. She moved her horse forward. "I'll not stop."

Then he beeped his car's horn loudly. Her horse was experienced and used to traffic and sudden noises, so he paid the sounds no mind. Tony drove beside her honking the horn and nudging the buggy while yelling out to her.

"Stop it! Stop it you maniac!" If she stopped the buggy, he would see she was pregnant and then things would be worse. If he didn't kill her, he might beat her and harm the baby. "Go away." She prayed and didn't know what else to do. The horse would never outrun the car, and she'd already left Amos's house and couldn't turn around because his car was alongside. Then she got an idea. "Okay I'll stop," she yelled out.

Once she stopped, he got out of the car, and was nearly at the buggy, she set the horse off racing. It would take him a while to get back to his car and start it again and by then she hoped to make it to the next house. He wouldn't kill her in front of people.

In her rear-view mirror, she could see him getting back in his car. She knew she was doomed. She prayed again for the safety of her baby. Then she heard galloping hooves from somewhere. She swiveled her head to the other side and saw Amos galloping on a horse and he was now beside her buggy.

"Stop!" he said.

With him there to protect her, she stopped. "Amos, it's Tony in the car."

"I'll handle him." He jumped off his horse and handed her a gun from out of his coat. "For protection," he said. Then he walked over to Tony who'd stopped a distance back from the buggy.

"I want to talk to Jeanie," Tony said to Amos. "Are you her boyfriend?"

"I'm a friend."

"What kind of friend?"

Jeanie heard them talking and wasn't brave

enough to look. She stared down at the gun and remembered Malachi teaching her the steps to use it.

"Leave the lady alone." Amos said.

"I just want to settle the score."

"What score would that be?"

"Get out of my way."

"I'm sorry, but I can't do that. You see, Jeanie is a good friend of mine."

"Is that right?"

"That is right. Jeanie is a friend to everybody in the Amish community."

"I might have to arrange for your disposal, too, just like her stupid husband."

Jeanie gasped when she heard those words. He had just admitted to killing Malachi, as plain as day. She looked down at the gun. She could step out of the buggy and shoot him right now, and if he hurt Amos she'd have to. The gun was heavier than the one she'd practiced with before. Malachi had told her everyone who lived on a farm had to know how to shoot.

"My place is just up the road there. Why don't we sit down and talk about this man-to-man?"

"I'm going to speak to Jeanie, not you."

"She doesn't want to speak to you."

Jeanie didn't want Tony to hurt Amos, so she decided to get out of the buggy. Tony could've had a gun in his pocket for all she knew. Just as she was getting out, a car came over the hill and she quickly got back in. Peeping over the buggy seat, she watched as Amos waved the car down. Then Tony got back in his car, reversed with a spin of his wheels, turned and screeched up the road. Amos asked the people to phone the police from one of their cell phones. When the call had been made, the car proceeded on its way.

Amos ran to her. "Are you all right, Jeanie?"

She took a deep breath. "Yes. Has he gone?"

"He has."

"He could've killed you, Amos."

"The police are on their way."

"He killed Malachi," Jeanie sobbed.

"Apparently so. Wait right there." He grabbed his patiently waiting horse and clipped his lead onto the back of the buggy. Then he opened the door and she moved over as he climbed into the driver's seat. "I'll take you back to my place. The police will be here soon."

"*Denke* for saving me."

She passed the gun back to him and he took it with his free hand. "At least you didn't have to use it."

"I was tempted. The police said they arrested him. I wonder what happened."

He gave a one-shoulder shrug, and she wondered if she would've actually used that gun.

As they waited in Amos's house for the police, Jeanie knew she wouldn't be able to carry on until she told Amos the whole truth.

"There's something else you need to know. I'm not the nice person you think I am, Amos."

"*Nee?* Then who are you?" He chuckled.

"I'm not joking, Amos. You might never want to speak with me again when you learn what I've done." She hoped he'd understand her desperation. "I deliberately came here weeks ago to … in a plot to win your heart."

He raised his eyebrows. "I'm flattered."

She shook her head. "You don't understand. Oh, Amos. I've fallen in love with you now, but back then I had nothing like that on my mind. I was only getting close to you so we could keep the farm."

He stared at her, shocked. "Tell me that again?"

"It's true."

"You didn't have feelings for me?"

She shook her head. "I didn't then, but I do now."

"You were deceiving me? Is that what you're saying?"

"Jah. That's exactly what I was doing."

He looked away. "How could you?"

He wasn't taking it as well as she'd hoped and she couldn't blame him. "I couldn't go on until I'd told you the truth."

"You might've told me the truth back then, before feelings developed."

"I didn't know how. I feel awful."

They heard a car and Amos stood and looked out the window. "It's the police. We'll talk about this when they've gone."

They found out from the police that Tony had slipped out of the station before they had been able to get that arrest warrant. Now they had the warrant and were looking for him. Jeanie and Amos told the police everything they knew, and all that Tony had said. The police asked them to go to the station the next morning to make official statements.

When the police left, Jeanie knew things had changed between Amos and herself. She could sense his disappointment. "I should go." She stood up.

"Wait. Let's talk."

"Okay." She sat down again hoping he wouldn't be too harsh.

"Do you mean to tell me you were wooing me in an attempt to have me fall in love with you so you could keep the farm?"

"Worse. As well, I hoped we'd marry to give my child security and a father."

He shook his head. "I'm sorry. I was wrong about you. I didn't think you'd be capable of doing that."

She looked into his dark eyes. "I'm not." She wanted to tell him that Magda had talked her into it. "I am, I guess, because that's what I did. But I couldn't live with myself. It was awful and I hope you'll forgive me."

"I forgive you, but I'll withdraw my offer of marriage."

She looked at him and he looked away from her. "I understand. I'm disappointed with myself. I understand how you feel."

"You can keep the farm. I'll have the papers re-drawn up into your name. I've asked them to go ahead with that anyway."

Jeanie stood. "I couldn't do that now, not after …"

"Jeanie, I want to give you the farm in memory of my good friend. As you once pointed out, it would've been yours if Malachi had lived."

"*Denke,* Amos, but I don't know. So much has happened. The farm's not the happy place it once was. It doesn't feel right to stay there now." She felt truly awful, and she had to get away. She stood up.

"I'll go now, and I'm dreadfully sorry things worked out like this."

He stood as well. "So am I. As you wish. We'll leave the farm as is." He walked to the door and she hurried to her buggy. "Wait, Jeanie."

She turned around. "You've had an awful fright. I'll take you home and I'll bring Werner back to drive the buggy home."

"*Denke.* I do feel a little shaken."

CHAPTER 22

SHE PREFERRED TO BE ALONE, but she had to think of the health of her baby. That was the only reason she agreed for Amos to drive her home. She was embarrassed about her behavior and everything she'd done. Desperation and fear had made her act against her principles.

FOR THE NEXT MONTHS, they kept working the farm. They hadn't talked with Amos and he hadn't talked with them. Zelda had left and there was no sign of her brothers. At the community gatherings they all avoided Amos, which was easy to do as he also avoided them.

. . .

Two weeks remained before her baby was due and Jeanie knew she had to put an end to the silliness. As the newly self-appointed head of their small household, she took it upon herself to straighten things out with Amos. It would be embarrassing to see him again, but it was important to her that things were sorted by the time the baby arrived. If he could allow them to stay until the potato harvest so they could see things through, then they'd find another place to live. Amos could do what he wanted with the farm. The three of them had become resigned to the fact that the farm would never be theirs.

Jeanie chose Saturday as the day. Neither Magda or Werner was home, so she could slip away unnoticed to visit Amos.

When she got closer to his house, she saw him bending down fixing a fence post close to the house. Jasper was by his side. Amos stood up when he saw her approach, and then he put Jasper behind the fence. She stopped the buggy and climbed out as he walked over.

"Morning, Jeanie."

"Hello, Amos. I wanted to have a word with you if I could?"

"Sure. Would you like to come inside?"

"We could sit on the porch. It's such a nice day."

He looked up at the morning sun making its way higher into the sky. "It's going to be a warm one." After he gave her a smile, they walked over to the porch. He sat on the far chair and she took the one closer.

It hit her suddenly, just how much she'd missed his company.

"I hope you haven't had any more trouble with that ex-boyfriend of yours?"

"*Nee*, he's keeping well away. He knows the police are keeping an eye on him. They told me he got bail and he's awaiting trial. Although, who knows how long that will be?"

"Good. I do worry about you."

"You do?" When he nodded, she stared into his dark eyes wondering if he missed her.

"I do. Are you surprised?"

She shrugged her shoulders. "A little, I guess. Things haven't been so good between us. I don't like to leave things the way they are. We haven't even discussed the farm and what will happen with it. I mean, it's yours to do with what you will."

"I no longer see the farm as mine, Jeanie. I've been leaving things as is because I'm embarrassed by my actions. That's why I haven't been to see you."

"You're embarrassed?"

"I am."

"So are we, and I hate that things are so awkward."

He shook his head and looked down.

"At one time, I cared so much about the farm because I thought I had to be strong for Werner and Magda. I was convinced Malachi wanted me to carry on and do what he would've done. Now I know that all he would've wanted was for me to be happy. Especially now that the baby's coming soon."

He was now smiling at her. "Have you been well?" When she nodded, he said, "All Malachi would've wanted was for you to be happy and your child to have a home where he could be raised."

"He?"

"Or she."

Jeanie giggled. "I know you're right and I wasted so much time and energy worrying about the future."

"I'm sorry, Jeanie. I was the one who caused you all that worry. I should've changed the contract to your name just like you said. My head was clouded, but now I see clearly. Anyway, the contract is now in your name and waiting for you to sign. I'll drive you there myself first thing Monday." He chuckled. "I'm convinced those lawyers think I'm crazy, what with all the changes I've instructed them to make, but I don't care."

She rubbed her head and looked away from him. "Are you sure that's what you want?"

"Jeanie, what I *want* is to marry you."

She whipped her head around to look back at him. "After all of my deception?"

"Don't be so hard on yourself. You were striving to help others, and you were right to tell me. I should've honored my word to Malachi right after he died, because … well, I just should've." He shrugged. "Tell me, is there any hope for you and me?"

This was the last thing she'd expected. "You mean, you still want to …"

"*Jah,* I still want to marry you, if you'll have me. One day, Werner will marry and he could take over the farm. Magda can stay there or live with us. Whatever you want, or wherever Magda wants to live. I can build on a *grossdaddi haus* here."

She looked down and pushed her fingertips into either side of her forehead, making tiny circles. "That's a lot to think about."

"I'm such a fool. Just answer me this."

Jeanie looked up, right into his dark chocolate-colored eyes. "What?"

"Do you have feelings for me?"

"I do."

"Why don't we marry, and then we can figure everything out from there?"

She could feel her face break into a smile. This talk had turned out better than she could've hoped. "I do miss you. I missed our Saturday's together." Now her child would have a father and a happy home.

"Will you give it some thought?"

"I will marry you, Amos. I don't need to give it any more thought."

His eyebrows flew nearly to his hat. "You will?"

Jeanie giggled. "I've felt so bad, sure that you thought me a dreadful person. Every day I was going over and over in my head how I could've — should've — done things differently. If you can overlook my faults, I'm happy to marry you."

The corners of his lips tilted upward. "Then, you'll overlook my faults?"

"I will." She was certain he didn't have many of those.

He jumped to his feet and lifted her up and encircled his arms around her and held her tight.

"Careful," she said with a giggle looking down at her baby bump. "You won't be able to hold me too close for a while." She felt a warm sensation spread down her legs and looked down at the liquid on the porch. "Oh! My water's broke."

He gasped. "Did I do that?"

"*Nee,* but the *boppli's* coming. Can you call Sandra Beiler?"

"*Jah,* are you okay?"

"I think so."

"Stay here." He ran to the barn.

"I'm not going anywhere," she said to herself as he disappeared behind the barn doors. She stood leaning on the porch rail, caressing her rounded belly and praying the birth would go all right. Nothing was as important as this baby coming into the world safely. It made her see that all those things she'd been worried about for the past months were nothing in comparison. A new life was coming and she had to be a good mother and teach her child right from wrong.

Looking up toward the barn, she saw Amos hurrying back. "She's twenty minutes away."

"Good."

"What can I do?"

"Nothing. I don't even have contractions yet." She was a little embarrassed about her water breaking in front of him, but that was something over which she'd had no control. Maybe it was a sign that she'd made the right choice when she'd accepted his proposal of marriage.

"Looks like you'll have the *boppli* under my roof — under our roof."

She smiled at him. "It seems when you give up and give everything over to *Gott,* He works things out."

He chuckled and stood beside her near the porch railing. "Someone said to me once that it's only when we stop worrying that *Gott* works on our problems for us."

When Jeanie felt a tightening of her abdomen, she touched the contraction with her hands. "I can feel something happening."

"Please wait until she comes. I've delivered horses and calves, but I think humans would be different."

Jeanie laughed. *"Jah,* those mothers wouldn't talk to you. I think you'll be safe if Sandra was only twenty minutes away."

He put his arm around her shoulders. "We've had a rocky start, you and I, but there's something about you that has always pulled me toward you."

"I feel it too. I enjoyed the time I've spent with you. I know we'll have a good life together."

"We need to be totally honest with each other."

"I agree," Jeanie said, glad they were of the same mind. "Can you call around and find out where Magda is? She wants to be at the birth."

"Sure."

Just when the midwife arrived, Jeanie had

another contraction. Soon after that, Sandra and Amos made up a room where Jeanie would have her baby.

Late that evening, at ten minutes past eleven, a baby boy came into the world. Jeanie took him into her arms with tears of joy and sadness, thinking about how happy Malachi would've been to see him. Magda hurried out of the room to let Amos know the baby had arrived safely. By now Magda had been told that Jeanie had accepted Amos's sudden proposal and she was delighted about it.

When Magda was back in the room, she leaned down and whispered in her ear, "When you're ready, we'll let Amos in to see him."

"When everything's cleaned up."

"Of course."

"Where's Werner?" Jeanie had been in too much pain to know if Werner had come to wait with Amos.

"Waiting at home to hear the news. Amos has just gone to the barn to call him."

"Good."

Magda stared down at the baby. "He looks just the same as Malachi."

Jeanie smiled at her mother-in-law's remark. She was certain newborn babies all looked similar.

Once the room had been cleaned and the baby was diapered and swaddled in a soft wrap, Sandra and Magda stepped out of the room, and Amos walked in. Jeanie looked up at him and smiled. "Here he is."

Amos walked closer. *"Are you okay?"*

"I am now. It was harder than I expected, and a little longer than I'd hoped."

Amos leaned down and kissed her forehead and then looked at the baby. "He's so beautiful, and so small. He's such a miracle."

"I know. I just can't stop staring at him. Look how perfect his fingernails are."

"Can I touch him? My hands are clean."

"Jah."

Amos leaned down and touched the baby's hand. "I've never been so close to a young *boppli* like this."

"You'll be his step*vadder* once we marry."

He chuckled and then she saw tears in his eyes. "I'm looking forward to it. We'll make it soon, *jah?"*

"I'd like that."

"I'll be the best *Dat* ever and the best husband."

"I know you will, you won't even have to try."

He leaned over and kissed her forehead. *"Denke,* for giving me a second chance."

"Seems like we've all been given a second chance."

Slowly, Amos nodded.

. . .

184

IT WAS five weeks later that Amos and Jeanie married. They had the ceremony at the potato farm.

After the wedding, Amos moved onto the farm with them. First, he made himself busy building onto the old house to make it bigger, and then he renovated the old section to make it nicer.

Magda and Werner were pleased that Jeanie and the baby hadn't moved away to Amos's house. And Amos enjoyed learning as much as he could about being a potato farmer. He was out in the fields most days working with Werner giving Magda and Jeanie the opportunity to stay in the house looking after the much-loved baby, Aaron.

Two years on.

A BABY SISTER, Patricia, arrived for Aaron, and soon after that, Werner became engaged to a girl from the same community. To keep him at the farm, Amos and Jeanie made plans for a second *haus* to be built on a plot of unused land behind the barn.

Jeanie never forgot her first husband, always grateful to God for having had Malachi in her life for those few short years. The man responsible for his death was now behind bars serving fifteen years. It wasn't long enough in Jeanie's mind, but she did her best not to focus on that. Detective Graeme had recently informed her that it was possible Tony would be charged with Booker's death, too, as their investigation had revealed tampering with the vehicle that had killed Malachi.

Jeanie left all of that in God's hands, and she enjoyed what she had today — a happy home, with those to whom she was closest.

Amos was grateful to *Gott* that Malachi had brought Jeanie to their community, and after Malachi's death, Jeanie had grown to love him as much as he loved her.

Five years on.

JEANIE WOKE when her husband gently shook her shoulder. She opened her eyes to see his worried face. "What is it?"

"We had a frost overnight."

She got up and hurried to the window to see a blanket of white covering their newly planted fields. The dark days she'd been through after Malachi's death had taught her a thing or two. "We'll do what we can to salvage the crop."

"I thought you'd be more upset."

Turning around, she looked into Amos's dark eyes. "How can I be? *Gott* has blessed me with so much. I have you and our *kinner*. How can I be upset over frost? Everything is just as *Gott* wants it, and that means *Gott* wanted there to be a frost. He always takes care of us." Through her dark years, she'd learned that everything worked out how it was meant to happen.

"I love you, Mrs. Troyer."

Jeanie giggled as her husband picked her up and spun her in a circle. She had finally learned that struggling and worrying were pointless when God was in charge. Everything that happened was already in God's perfect and loving plan, so why was there a need to worry? They would do what they could, knowing He would always take care of them.

Thank you for reading The Amish Potato Farmer's Widow. I hope you enjoyed it.

To stay up to date with my new releases and special offers, add your email at my website in the newsletter section.

https://samanthapriceauthor.com/

Or add your email here :

http://eepurl.com/dKZ5WQ

Blessings,

Samantha Price

THE NEXT BOOK IN THE SERIES:

Amish Widow's Tears.

Can she trust her broken heart?

Is he lying?

When Amish woman, Millie, was suddenly widowed, she learned how hard it was alone. She wasn't alone for long before her daughter was born.

Life got even more complicated when a man joined their Amish community. He made his interest in Millie quite clear, but it's too soon to think about another man.

Apart from that, she's not sure about him. Is he being honest with her about everything?

Will loneliness and despair cloud Millie's judge-ment and cause her to make a hasty decision?

Is Millie about to make the biggest mistake of her life?

You will love this poignant story of love, survival, and grace.

Amish Widow's Tears.

EXPECTANT AMISH WIDOWS SERIES

Book 1 Amish Widow's Hope

Book 2 The Pregnant Amish Widow

Book 3 Amish Widow's Faith

Book 4 Their Son's Amish Baby

Book 5 Amish Widow's Proposal

Book 6 The Pregnant Amish Nanny

Book 7 A Pregnant Widow's Amish Vacation

Book 8 The Amish Firefighter's Widow

Book 9 Amish Widow's Secret

Book 10 The Middle-Aged Amish Widow

Book 11 Amish Widow's Escape

Book 12 Amish Widow's Christmas

Book 13 Amish Widow's New Hope

Book 14 Amish Widow's Story

Book 15 Amish Widow's Decision

Book 16 Amish Widow's Trust

Book 17 The Amish Potato Farmer's Widow

Book 18 Amish Widow's Tears

ABOUT SAMANTHA PRICE

USA Today Bestselling author, Samantha Price, wrote stories from a young age, but it wasn't until later in life that she took up writing full time. Formally an artist, she exchanged her paintbrush for the computer and, many best-selling book series later, has never looked back.

Samantha is happiest on her computer lost in the world of her characters. She is best known for the Ettie Smith Amish Mysteries series and the Expectant Amish Widows series.

www.SamanthaPriceAuthor.com

Samantha loves to hear from her readers. Connect with her at:

samantha@samanthapriceauthor.com
www.facebook.com/SamanthaPriceAuthor
Follow Samantha Price on BookBub
Twitter @ AmishRomance
Instagram - SamanthaPriceAuthor